The Ragged Urchin

Lynette Rees

© Lynette Rees 2018
Contact Lynette:
http://www.lynetterees.com
Blogs:
https://lynetterees.wordpress.com/
http://www.nettiesramblings.blogspot.com
email: lynetterees@mail.com
Facebook author page for latest updates:
http://www.facebook.com/authorlynetterees/

Acknowledgement
to Helen Snow

Many thanks for your invaluable help and support with this book. You have a keen eye for detail and a knack for knowing how I like the story to flow. I appreciate the time you have given up to knock this story into shape!

Dedication

For all those Victorian children who had no choice other than to sacrifice their childhoods to work in dangerous and often deadly conditions. May your little souls find peace.

Chapter One
Early autumn 1873 London, England

The small dark wood coffin in the corner of the room was somehow swamped by the people surrounding it. Ten-year-old Archie Ledbetter gulped as he stared at all the people packed into the tiny shabby living room with its peeling wallpaper and threadbare rugs. Surrounded by a sea of black he felt like a tiddler in amongst a large shoal of fish. Who were half of them anyhow? He didn't know. All he knew was the one person who had taken care of him all his life was now fast asleep and as cold as ice in that wooden box over there. Where had that beautiful smile she possessed disappeared to? How could someone as full of life as his mother, now be dead? It couldn't possibly be true. Any moment now he'd wake up to find her at the bottom of his bed tickling his toes as she usually did, her eyes shining like two stars in the sky, as she said, 'Get up, sleepy head! There's a big bowl of porridge on the table downstairs for you. Get washed, dressed, fed and out of the door for school today!'

He didn't have a father but that hadn't seemed to matter much, though he had a vague recollection of a man who called to the house when he was much younger. The strange thing was the man never came during the hours of daylight only at night. He'd once glimpsed him and his ma locked in an embrace when he'd stood at the top of the stairs watching through the railings of the wooden bannister, but she'd never mentioned him to Archie and now he wondered who that man was. Not having a father though hadn't seemed that much of a deal to him, not until the other lads at school began to rib him about it. 'Oi, shorthouse, where's your dad?', 'Archie, Archie, titchy lad, whatever happened to yer bleedin' dad?' Taunts like that had upset him and made him cry, but he hadn't wanted to show Ma. There'd even been a schoolyard rumour that his mother had been 'knocked up' by one of the members of the gentry at a very grand house. But no one was able to fill him in on the name or details about the house or family. And when he'd asked his mother who his father was, she never gave him a satisfactory answer. One day she'd say something like, 'He's someone you're never likely to meet, so forget all about him, Archie,' or another time she'd say, 'We don't need to talk about him, we're fine as we are!'

Then she'd ruffle his hair, plant a big sloppy kiss on his cheek and ask him to make toffee dabs with her in the scullery, allowing him the biggest one to eat afterwards.

It was one of the ways she'd made a living, making things from home and selling them. She had a little market stall selling her confectionary and cakes and spoke of one day owning her own shop.

'Someday, Archie,' she'd say with one arm draped around his shoulder, and the other raised as she pointed to the wall, 'It will bear our names over the door! Rose Ledbetter and Son, retailers of confectionary and cakes!'

Then she'd turned him around to face her with a big gleam in her eyes. He could still smell her parma violet perfume if he closed his eyes to think of her. 'You do believe me, don't you, son?'

And he'd nodded at the time, knowing how much she'd wanted it and realising how much she'd loved him. Then she'd clutched him to her breast and sobbed as she'd said, 'I'm doing this for you, son!'

But he didn't understand why she was crying? Surely it was something to be happy about not sad? That she had great plans for the future and to make them both rich!

He jolted out of his memory as he caught a snippet of conversation behind him, that seemed to be coming from a pair of elderly women he vaguely recognised huddled in the corner.

'It was such a shock when it 'appened though, Martha. We all thought Alicia was as fit as a flea…'

'But what's to become of the boy?' He heard the other woman say in a whisper.

'His uncle is coming to collect him later and taking him to stay at his home, Ginny just told me.'

His uncle? That's was the first he'd heard of it. Would it be Uncle Walter or Uncle Herbert? He preferred Herbert as he was always so full of fun and a regular to the house. He also loved Auntie Marge's jam and cream scones. He always got a warm welcome at their modest home. But Uncle Walter he barely knew. He hadn't seen him since last Christmas, the man had never married and barely smiled. He hoped that wasn't the uncle the women spoke of.

'What are you doing all on yer own, child?' It was the voice of his next-door neighbour, Ginny, breaking into his thoughts. She'd been taking care of him since his ma'd died. He gulped and looking up at her, wiped a tear away.

She smiled and hugged him to her. 'Sorry, I went missing for a moment there, Archie. I had to go outside to see if the undertaker had arrived and got caught out by Mrs Mack from across the street who wanted all the gen from me. 'Course, I never gave her any. Why should she know all the ins and outs when she can't be bothered to call to the house and pay her respects, today of all days?'

She pulled away and took his small hand in her rather larger one. He curled his fingers around her warm hand. Ginny's hands always seemed as warm as her heart.

'Now, I'll tell you what's goin' to happen, shall I?'

He nodded, his eyes glistening with tears, his stomach jittery and unsettled as he sensed that his life was about to change forever.

Ginny took a deep breath and let it out again, then she ran a hand through her flame-red hair. 'The funeral procession will leave the house in a few minutes. Your mother's coffin will be placed in the horse-drawn hearse and the rest of us will walk behind it. The church is only a couple of streets away, so there won't be much walkin' for us to do. Not enough to tire us out at any rate. Now be a good lad as I tell everyone what's going to happen, won't you?'

He nodded again just as a fat tear rolled down his cheek and he tasted its saltiness.

'Here yer are, lad…' Ginny slipped her hand into her skirt pocket and handed him her embroidered handkerchief. 'It is clean, I have another in me other pocket. Now dry yer eyes and blow your nose!' she commanded.

He did as told hoping no one would notice, but thankfully, they were all too busy muttering amongst themselves to pay heed to him.

Archie swallowed hard as he found himself surging forward in amongst the crowd to the street outside, where a black hearse attached to two black horses with feathered plumage, stood ready to receive his mother's coffin. He felt so lost in amongst it all.

'Paid for by her rich brother,' he heard a man in the crowd say, but when he turned around he couldn't work out which man had said it as there were so many wearing black hats and jackets. His rich uncle was Uncle Walter. He'd often wondered about him and how come he was wealthy when his mother was poor. Uncle Herbert, though, wasn't his real uncle at all. Herbert and Marge were good friends of his mother's. So why did Ma say he was? He could never work that one out.

But there was no sign of Uncle Walter at the funeral. Why was that? Then he heard the same male voice say, 'Bet he wouldn't lower himself to come here today after all she did to her family. Disgraced the Brookings she did!'

What could his ma have possibly done to disgrace the Brookings? Wasn't that Uncle Walter's surname? It was all a mystery to him.

Archie turned again to see the men were holding their bowler hats and flat caps to their chests. Then he noticed it. Two men in black top hats and long coats carrying his mother's coffin. The men looked very serious, no one smiled and the crowd seemed to bow their heads in unison. He gulped. When he'd been inside he somehow managed to pretend the coffin was part of the furniture, it was the only way he could cope with it all, but out here, his mother's coffin looked more real somehow. The polished mahogany wood, gleaming gold name plaque and matching handles made his stomach flip over.

He heard someone let out a low whistle. 'I bet that cost a bob or two…'

Then a high-pitched woman's voice said, 'She must have broken 'er parents' hearts running off like that…'

'Sssh, Martha, the boy will hear you. It's a secret that's best left buried…' Another woman spoke in hushed tones.

A secret? He never knew his mother had kept any secrets at all, but then again she was never willing to tell him who his father was and he didn't appear to have any grandparents like his friends did. How he'd envied them that.

'She always had big ideas that one mind…' the woman carried on. 'Thought she was better than the rest of us—The Duchess of Dock Street!'

'Show some respect, Martha, for goodness sake, Alicia hasn't even been laid to rest yet.'

Archie turned and glared at the woman, causing her face to redden and she turned away in shame.

'See, now look what yer've gorn and done, you've spilt the beans and the boy has overheard you.' Then in a louder voice. 'She didn't mean nothing by it Archie, your ma was a lovely lady.'

He managed a smile. Later he would ask Ginny what it was all about but for time being there was a burial to attend.

Chapter Two

'For as much as it has pleased our Heavenly Father in His wise providence to take unto Himself our beloved Alicia May Ledbetter, we therefore commit her body to the ground. Earth to earth, ashes to ashes, dust to dust…' the vicar was saying as he sprinkled some earth onto the coffin that had been lowered into the earth. Archie could barely take it all in. He felt like letting go of Ginny's hand and jumping into the grave alongside his ma. He couldn't believe her body would be left in that cold ground and she would never again be coming home with him. She'd loved this church, it had meant something to her and she'd never missed a Sunday service until she became ill. Her faith seemed to have got her through some difficult times and there had been plenty of those.

A wind whipped up as he stood at the graveside, his eyes blurring with tears as the vicar's voice seemed to fade as Archie's own thoughts intruded.

'Our Father, who art in heaven…'

Father, if you really are in heaven, please take care of my ma. Archie clutched the red rose Ginny had given him in his hand, so hard that he felt its pricks dig into his palm, but he didn't care. He needed to feel the pain to prove this was real.

'Go ahead,' Ginny whispered. He knew it was his cue to drop his rose onto the coffin before the grave diggers covered his mother's grave with earth. It was the last thing he could give her, a red rose covered in his blood. He tossed the rose and watched it fall atop the coffin. He swallowed hard, that lump he'd had in his throat was getting bigger threatening to choke him.

As they left the cemetery grounds of St. Luke's Church, Ginny put her hand on Archie's shoulder. 'You've been a big brave boy,' she said. He could hear her ragged breaths as if the day had been difficult for her. 'And I'm so proud of you.' Then she knelt to hug him to her breast as people walked past in silence dodging headstones and the sticking out branches of yew trees and overgrown bushes that got in their way.

'What's going to happen to me now?' he asked, fearful for his future.

'I've been given instructions that you are to move in with your Uncle Walter…'

He shook his head and began to cry. 'Can't I stay with you?' he pleaded.

The kindness in Ginny's eyes reflected what she felt for the lad. She wiped away her own tears. 'I'm afraid you can't, Archie. I can't afford to feed another mouth under my roof and you're a bit young to go out to work.'

'But I would work for you and all,' he said, brightening up.

'Aye, I guess you would and all, lad,' she smiled, 'but you'll not earn enough to pay yer keep. It's much better for you to go to live with your Uncle Walter. It was your mother's wish. He has agreed to take you on and by all accounts, he has a lovely house. You'll want for nothing. Yer'll end up a right little lord, you see if you don't!' She rose to her feet.

He shook his head vigorously. 'Well, I don't much fancy that!'

'I'm only teasing you, Archie. If you go to live with your uncle, it means nothing of the kind, just that yer'll have a better life than if you stay living around here with the likes of us!'

But he didn't want to leave the likes of Ginny and her family, nor his Uncle Herbert and Auntie Marge who weren't his real auntie and uncle but were close to him anyhow. He looked at Ginny, who was now dabbing at her eyes with a handkerchief. 'Why isn't my Uncle Walter here today for my mother's funeral?'

Ginny shook her head. 'Maybe it was too painful for him. All I've been told is he's on business in the city today and he's sending his carriage over to collect you later. I've packed all your clothes for you, but I expect he'll buy you new.'

'But why can't I stay at home?' he persisted.

'Because yer too young to look after yerself and you won't be able to pay the rent. There's something I must tell you…' Her eyes were darting all over the place.

Why was Ginny looking so sheepish? It wasn't like her, and why did he feel this was very bad news for him?

'Pardon?'

'You won't be able to return to your house before you leave, the landlord's moving a new family into yours.'

He felt as if the ground was coming up to meet him, nothing felt safe any more. 'How can that be?'

'Because your ma had fallen behind with the rent money, Archie, as the doctor's fees had to be paid. You have to see it from the landlord's point of view. He can't allow people to live in his houses free of charge.'

'But Ma was doing well. She told me so, we were going to have a shop together someday.'

Ginny closed her eyes for a moment and then opened them again. 'Aw, Archie, it was a pipe dream that's all, things people say and hope for that will never come true…'

His eyes glazed over. Ginny had to be lying to him. He knew his mother had been telling the truth, she wouldn't tell a fib. He pulled away from the woman's embrace and pushing past the last of the stragglers in the cemetery, made for his house, past several busy streets, carts and vagabonds until he reached number sixteen Dock Street. If he went in there now he was sure Ma would be waiting for him, dressed in her blue pinafore with his tea on the table. It was all one big joke. It couldn't be real. He was brought up sharp as the front door blew open to reveal a strange man there scratching his head. Where was Ma? The man looked like many other dockers in the area that had settled in these parts. But he'd never seen this particular man before in his life.

''Ave yer seen a fella with a horse and cart, lad?' The man looked at him then up and down the street.

Archie shook his head. What was he doing inside his home?

'He should have been 'ere with me furniture by now, we're moving in today, see. Poor lady who was living in this house died and hadn't paid the rent by all accounts, but her misfortune was our gain,' he grinned and winked at Archie. Then as if sensing something was amiss, he asked, 'Did you know the lady, Alice Ledbetter, then?'

Not wanting to embarrass the man, who seemed quite nice, Archie shook his head. 'No, sir, I didn't.' *Silly man, her name is Alicia!*

'Well, anyway lemme know if yer out playing in the street and yer see the cart, it might have gone to the wrong house, see.'

Archie nodded and, stuffing his hands in the pockets of his breeches, walked away.

***

Darkness had descended by the time Archie realised he should have gone back to find Ginny, but somehow he didn't care. What did anything matter any more? All he cared about right now was staying where he was and not with some strange uncle in a big house who appeared miserable as sin!

It was then he noticed a large carriage parked at the end of his street with the driver sat on top. Ginny suddenly appeared running around frantically waving her arms in mid air.

'Archie! There you are! I've been worried about you, sweetheart! Your uncle has sent his carriage to take you to his home. I've got yer things packed for you to leave.'

Archie frowned. 'I don't want to leave you, ever, Ginny!' He threw himself into her arms and they both wept together.

'I'm sorry, lad, you have to go, but I've no doubt you'll be back to see me again, all toffed up like a lord!'

'I will come back someday. Please though, if I don't like living with that uncle I don't really know, please can I come to live with you?'

She bit her lip, obviously unsure what to say to him. 'I'm sure you'll love it in that beautiful big house so much so that you'll forget all about yer Auntie Ginny next door!'

'Never!' he said with conviction because he meant it.

'I'll just nip inside and get yer clobber, lad,' she said, leaving him standing on the pavement staring at the shiny carriage beside him with the very prim and proper driver sitting atop of it. He wore a top hat on his head just like the undertaker had done at his Ma's funeral.

Soon Ginny returned with a bundle of his clothes tied up in a knotted bed sheet. 'I've made you some jam tarts for your journey, Archie,' she said. 'Not as good as yer Ma's, of course, but yer'll enjoy them all the same!'

She signalled to the driver he was ready to leave and kissed Archie softly on the cheek.

He was going to miss kindly, warm-hearted Ginny from next door. He wondered what lay ahead of him.

**

The ride to his uncle's home seemed to be never-ending, as the coach rattled across cobbles and roads with heavy traffic, that gave way to winding country lanes and hedgerows. What kind of life would he have now? The high life didn't particularly appeal to him, he'd much rather be playing marbles or pitch and toss in Dock Street. Finally, they arrived outside a large, imposing building which was impossible to have much impression of during the hours of darkness.

The cab driver opened the door for Archie. 'Cor, sir, are you sure this is where I'm supposed to be?' he asked, eyes wide with surprise.

'Yes, I can assure you that this is the home of your Uncle, Mr Walter Brooking...This is Huntington Hall, young man.'

Archie gulped as he was led not to the back door of the property as he was expecting for someone of the likes of him but to the front instead where they were met by a thin woman, who had her nose in the air. She wore a long dress with a white lace collar. 'The boy, Archibald, has arrived, Mrs Linley,' the cab driver informed her. He gave Archie a little prod for him to step forward so she could observe him.

'Hmmm, looks all skin and bone to me,' the woman said narrowing her gaze. 'Ten-years-old and scrawny and all. We'll have to get Cook to feed you up, my lad! Polly, the housemaid, will give you a good scrub as well!'

She's a fine one to talk! Archie thought. He couldn't believe how she tagged him "all skin and bone" when she was so skinny herself.

She glanced at him. 'Suppose you're hungry, boy?'

He shrugged. Truth be told, with all the sadness of the day's events, for once he wasn't particularly hungry at all but he didn't want to offend anyone. 'Come with me and we'll get you sorted. Thank you, Hodgekiss.'

So that was the driver's name, Mr Hodgekiss.

He was led in from the front step, through a large mahogany panelled door and taken down a fancy, dimly lit hallway which was adorned with marble heads on podiums rather like he'd once seen at the museum. Framed landscaped paintings and portraits decorated the walls and he wondered if some of those folk were his relations?

He thought he heard the mumbling of men's voices in the distance coming from one room but the housekeeper carried on walking.

Finally, they arrived at a door which Mrs Linley pushed open with one hand to reveal kitchen counters and clouds of steam. By the delicious smells wafting beneath his nose, he realised he was in the heart of the house. And by the sight of the large-bosomed woman with the twinkly blue eyes stood before him, he guessed she was the boss of this place.

'This is young Archibald, the master's nephew,' Mrs Linley said in a clipped matter of fact manner. 'He's come to live here with his uncle as he's recently been orphaned.'

Orphaned? No one had ever described him as an orphan before, what did that mean?

'Is he now?' Cook said, as she patted him on the head. 'I'm Mrs Stockley, lad. Pleased to make your acquaintance. Now sit down there by the fire and I'll take your bundle from you.'

He nodded. He would never dream of disagreeing with his elders, anyhow. That wasn't the way he'd been brought up. He'd been raised to listen to what they told him and to act accordingly. But in truth, he'd never minded anything his mother had asked of him. She'd been kindness itself. He'd feared his teachers at school though but realised it was all in the name of discipline. Spare the rod and spoil the child as it were. That was written in big letters on the wall in the hall at school.

'By heck, lad, you could do with a right good scrub!'

Archie turned to see a young girl wearing a mobcap and starched white apron stood before him. He guessed she was about fifteen-years-old.

'Sorry,' he muttered. 'After the fun'ral I went out running around the streets and got myself grimy.'

'Well, it won't do for you to meet the master looking like that,' Cook said sharply. 'Go and fill the bath for him, Polly. You can give him a good scrub with a bar of that lye soap. There's some in the scullery left over from washing the clothes.'

'What if he's got nits, Cook?' Polly blinked as if the thought had only just occurred to her.

'Well, if he has them we'll just have to deal with it, girl!' She rolled her eyes then winked at Archie. 'Polly'll get you clean after I've given you a cup of tea and a piece of my fruit cake. I daresay you can manage some, lad?'

Fruit cake? He hadn't even eaten one of Ginny's jam tarts as yet.

He gulped.

'What's the matter, boy? I've never had anyone turn down one of my cakes as yet!'

'It's just Ginny made me some tarts and I haven't had time to eat those yet. Haven't much felt like it to tell the truth.'

'After what happened today?' Cook asked with kindly blue eyes the colour of cornflowers he's once seen in a field. 'I heard all about what happened to your ma and why you're coming to live here. Now don't be bothered about that cake. It'll keep. Have a couple of Jenny's tarts instead.'

'Ginny,' he corrected.

'All right, Ginny then. Who's she? Anyhow?'

'Me old neighbour next door. She was right friendly to me and Ma.'

Cook quirked a brow as she placed one hand over the other, then pursed her lips. 'I bet she was and all.' Then turning to the maid, said in a strident tone, 'Come along, Polly. Go pour the lad a nice cuppa and I'll fetch a plate for his jam tarts. Then you can bathe him afterwards. Put the water on the range to boil, we haven't got all night you know!'

Polly shook her head and gazed heavenwards. No doubt she was used to getting lots of orders fired at her from Cook. There was no larking about in her kitchen – that was a cert.

Archie could hardly believe the plate Polly handed to him. It was very delicate, adorned with colourful roses and had a fancy gold edging. He'd not seen anything as grand in all his life. At home, they'd only acquired a few chipped cups and plates and not one of them matched either.

'Best bone china!' Polly explained. 'Watch you don't drop it mind, else Cook will have your guts for garters!'

'I'll be careful,' he mumbled.

'Where's your jam tarts, anyhow?'

He pulled a small knotted handkerchief from his jacket pocket and unwrapped it to reveal the tarts, which by now had gone a bit squishy.

'Hurry up and put them on the plate. We don't want no crumbs on the bleedin' floor!' Polly said sharply. And then, as if realising she was being short with him said, 'I'll do it for you, Archie, shall I?'

He nodded. 'Yes please, Polly.'

She smiled at him and at that point he realised he'd won both her and the cook over. But he'd yet to encounter the master of the house so far and the last time he had, the man had been very sullen indeed and had barely spoken to him at all.

***

'Cor, lad, you need a good scrub and all!' Polly shrieked as her hands flew to her face. 'Didn't anyone ever give you a good wash? You could grow a crop of potatoes in those flamin' lugholes!'

'Yes, me ma used to bathe me in an old tin bath and I was a lot cleaner earlier today, honest I was, but I've been out around the streets. I didn't want to leave me home and come here...'

'Aw, I'm sorry, lad. I forgot. Cook told me yer ma passed away and today was the funeral.'

He nodded.

'Are you very sad?' she said, passing him a big white fluffy towel to dry himself with.

'I am, yes, miss. I can't understand it. Nothing seems to make sense. I can't believe she's gone.' To his horror, he felt tears prick his eyes. He didn't want to look like a little boy in front of Polly.

'I'm sorry. I didn't want to make you cry,' She soothed as she took the towel from him and began to pat him down gently with it.

He sniffed back a sob then took a deep breath. 'You haven't. I'm all right really.' He didn't want to cry in front of the girl, there'd be time for that when he was alone later.

'What happened to her?'

He shrugged. 'She was all right a few weeks back. But then she got sick with a fever. But I always thought she'd get better.'

Polly tossed the used towel to one side, then handed Archie a flannel nightshirt to put on. She stood there sympathetically, with a large tortoiseshell comb in her hand ready to comb his hair. 'Did anyone call the doctor?'

'Yes, Ginny next door did. She got a doctor out. She had to pay him and all, nearly all the money me Ma had saved up from working at the market. But in the end, it didn't do much good.' He rubbed his nose.

Cook entered the room. 'Haven't you got the boy sorted yet?' She asked, winking at Archie.

'He was just telling me what happened to his ma, Mrs Stockley.'

Cook let out a loud harrumph and glared at the maid. 'Polly Matthews, you shouldn't be interrogating the poor boy at a time like this! Don't you realise what a difficult day it's been for him?' She wagged a finger at her.

Archie didn't want to get the girl into trouble. 'I don't mind, honestly, Mrs Stockley. I just told Polly how me ma got sick and one day could no longer get out of bed...'

He looked at Cook in earnest.

'Sometimes these things happen and gawd knows why...' Cook rolled up the sleeves of her dress. 'But your mother's in a better place now, you can be sure of that, Archie.'

He nodded, sniffed, then wiped away a tear with the back of his hand.

'Get that nightshirt on, lad,' Polly said, as if she wanted him to think about something else.

Cook whispered something in Polly's ear. They exchanged glances, then Polly said, 'Well, I'll be off as I have other things to be doing. Mrs Stockley will take over.' She smiled at Archie and patted his shoulder before leaving the room.

'Here you are, Archie,' Cook said handing him a flannelette dressing gown. 'Put this on and I've got you a pair of slippers. I reckon they should fit, they're old ones the master used to wear when he was about your age. Then once you're dressed, I'll make us a cup of cocoa and we'll have a nice little chat about things.'

Before the roaring fire that crackled and spat in the hearth, Cook explained something to him. 'It's about your Uncle Walter.'

Archie sat forward in his armchair with avid interest, arching his brows with curiosity as he did so.

'He and your ma fell out a long time ago...'

'You knew my mother?' He sat back in his chair.

'Yes, lad, I did.'

'What was she like when you knew her, Mrs Stockley?' Apart from Uncle Walter, he hadn't known anyone who'd known his mother when she was young.

Mrs Stockley's eyes glazed over as she rocked in her chair by the fireside. 'She was adorable. She had long golden locks and bright blue eyes, oh and a smile that fair nearly lit up the room. She was such a sweet child, an absolute angel. Her and your Uncle Walter made this house ring with their laughter. They had great childhoods.'

Archie wondered what could possibly have happened to make his uncle so miserable and moody and his mother to leave her lovely home? Did he dare ask?

But before he had a chance to say anything, Polly entered the room nursing a stone hotwater bottle in her arms. 'I think it's time I showed this young fellow to his bedroom. What do you say, Mrs Stockley?'

Cook nodded. 'Aye, it is getting late.' She turned to Archie and looking him in the eyes said, 'Your uncle has requested you have his old bedroom, it's in the north wing, facing the woods. We'll speak again some other time.' Then her eyes glazed over once more as if she was lost in the memory of a bygone era.

Archie shifted out of his armchair and followed Polly as they left the kitchen and climbed the highly polished, curved staircase to bed. He'd never seen such a grand staircase before, mahogany and long and winding. And to the side of it was an oval window so high that no one would be able to reach it even if they stood on tiptoes. He should have been sleepy but his mind was working overtime. There seemed to be more questions than answers about this house and it made him feel uncomfortable. If only some of those portraits could speak.

Chapter Three

Archie woke bright and early the following morning as Polly tapped his bedroom door. 'Now, I've got your day clothes laid out for you in the dressing room next door,' she said brightly as she breezed in. 'I trust you slept well?' She drew back the fancy yellow drapes.

He yawned and nodded. It had been a long while until he'd dropped off to sleep during the night as he kept seeing his mother's face and wondering what she was like as a young girl and what Uncle Walter had been like too. He just couldn't have imagined his uncle being a young boy, nor his mother being a young girl for that matter, never mind them being brother and sister. But once he had fallen asleep he'd been dead to the world.

He pulled himself up into a sitting position and got out of bed, rushing over to the window Polly had just opened to allow some fresh air into the room. Outside he saw acres of woodland and a farmer in a nearby field. There wasn't much noise out here, save for the chirping of the birds. Back in the East End he'd have heard people's voices, the costermongers and traders of the day beginning work, it was always so rowdy where he'd lived. Suddenly, he felt a sharp pang of pain as he remembered why he was here and now his mother was gone, buried beneath the cold sod and his Aunt Ginny was no longer in his life either.

He sighed loudly causing Polly to turn and look at him in alarm. 'What's the matter with you, Archie?'

'I was just thinking about yesterday…'

'Try not to trouble yourself so. Today you are to have breakfast with your uncle so hurry up and get washed and dressed.' She poured some water from a flowered jug on the wooden vanity unit into a matching basin and handed him a bar of white soap.

'But I had a good scrub last night!' he protested.

'That may be so, my lad, but in this house, we wash at least once a day!'

Before she had a chance to scrub his face for him, he picked up the awaiting flannel and dipped it in the warm water, rubbed on the soap, then scrubbed his face being careful not to get any in his eyes.

'Come on, you can do better than that! You've only had a cat's lick there. Wash behind your ears and your neck too!' she scolded.

He grinned. In some ways it was nice having people to fuss over him once again.

She handed him the towel then pointed to the door of an adjoining room he'd never noticed before. 'Go in there and get dressed!' she commanded. Although she sounded very bossy he knew her bark was worse than her bite, so he did as asked.

The adjoining room was smaller than his bedroom, with a large oak wardrobe, a chair and a small table. His clothing was set out neatly on the table.

'But where's my old clothes?' He blinked in confusion.

'Cook thought it best to burn those. You won't be needing them any more, you'd look out of place in them here,' Polly explained.

He was about to protest, but then thought better of it. He looked at the new garments before him. There was a frilly white shirt, which he thought would make him look like a girl. Surely there was some mistake? A pair of grey breeches, matching jacket and a smart cap. He looked at Polly as if for confirmation this was what he was to wear.

She smiled and nodded. 'Not what you're used to, I guess?'

He shook his head. He didn't want to look like no nob, he remembered what Ginny had said to him about being toffed up like a lord.

'Hurry up, we can't keep the master waiting,' Polly urged, as she helped him off with his nightshirt. Within minutes he had dressed and she led him to a walnut encased full-length mirror in the corner of the bedroom. He screwed up his face when he saw himself and blinked several times. Disbelieving the reflection was his own.

'Quite the young gent, aren't you, Archie? I've seen a painting of the master when he was your age and you look rather alike.'

The ruffles from the frills on his shirt scratched his neck and the breeches and jacket felt stiff and starchy, not like his well-worn kegs at home. But he had to go along with it. Now time to meet his uncle.

A short while later he was stood outside the dining room with its large dark wood doors as Polly knocked, then opened them announcing his presence.

'Enter!' boomed his uncle.

Archie blinked to see him seated at one end of the longest polished table he'd ever seen in his life before. Polly gave him a push so he stood at the other end of the table which had also been set for someone to dine.

His uncle, who had bushy sideburns and wavy brown hair, looked at him, his grey eyes giving nothing away. 'Archibald,' he said. 'Sit down, young man.'

Archie nodded and Polly drew out a chair for him to be seated.

'Say nothing unless spoken to,' she hissed in his ear.

He wouldn't have known what to say in any case.

'Give him a bowl of porridge!' Walter said, addressing Polly. 'Then he can have some kippers and bread and butter, he needs feeding up.'

A butler entered carrying a folded up newspaper on a round silver tray which he presented to Archie's uncle.

There was no more conversation after that. His uncle, who had already finished breakfasting which was evident by the crumbs and fish bones still on his plate, proceeded to read the newspaper and ignore Archie, whilst Archie tentatively ate his breakfast. Would it be like this at every meal time, he wondered? The man acting like he wasn't there?

A few minutes later, his uncle folded the newspaper.

This is it, Archie thought. At last, he is going to speak to me. But he discarded it on the table, rose and left the room as if Archie wasn't there at all. Had he done something wrong? Something to upset Uncle Walter? He wasn't quite sure.

Later he asked Cook when he'd located the kitchen. Everything looked different in daylight, so it took him some time to find the place.

Cook was in the middle of rolling out a thick wedge of pastry, her floured hands rolling the wooden pin back and forth meticulously. 'Aw, don't take notice, Archie. He's always the same, hardly speaks to any of us, unless he has to. I should have warned you about him.'

'But why is he like that, Mrs Stockley?' Archie rested his elbows on the counter as he watched Cook at work. He'd loved doing the same when his ma was baking at home.

'I don't rightly know, but one thing I can tell you is that he means no harm by it, he's just not very communicative that's all. Doesn't show his feelings either. I know he didn't attend your mother's funeral yesterday, but he did give you some thought by arranging for you to stay here. So hang on to that. He's not got the heart of steel that folk think. Remember I knew him when he was a young boy. Something happened to make him that way, and one day, when you're older I'll explain. But for time being, just accept him as he is.'

Archie nodded. Didn't make any sense to him. The delicious smells wafting his way from the oven made his stomach growl with hunger. In the event, he'd hardly touched his breakfast as he'd thought his uncle had something against him but obviously that just wasn't true.

'Want to try one of my pies?' Cook offered as she laid down her rolling pin for the moment.

Archie straightened up and nodded. 'Yes, please, Mrs Stockley.'

'We're having the chimneys swept here this week, so tomorrow morning, Mr Brackley, Polly's uncle, will be arriving with a young lad, so don't be alarmed if you see one big fella and a little boy as black as the ace of spades, will you, Archie?'

He shook his head. He'd seen enough sweeps around the place to know what they were and all. There'd been plenty around the East End.

Cook moved over to the stove and carefully opened the oven door using a thick piece of towelling not to burn herself. She placed the tray of pies on the counter beside her. Then used a wooden spatula to slip one of the smaller pies on a plate for Archie. It was oozing with thick gravy escaping from inside it, and he inhaled the steam as his mouth moistened in anticipation of what was to come.

'Mind as it's very hot,' she warned, as she handed him a knife and fork. 'Take a seat at the table.'

'Thanks, Mrs Stockley,' he said, as he seated himself. She hadn't even insisted he wash his hands, so he said nothing.

He blew on the pie but seeing Cook's face, cut it into small pieces to allow it to cool, before shovelling forkfuls into his mouth.

'My, my, I've never seen a lad eat like you before!' she chuckled, 'but I have to admit your ma obviously brought you up well as you have excellent manners!' She patted his head. No one had ever told him that before and it made him feel good inside to be praised like that.

Polly breezed into the kitchen carrying a silver tray of used crockery and cutlery. She blew back a strand of hair from her face. 'That Mrs Pearson has been here again and she's made short work of your fondant fancies, Mrs Stockley!'

Cook tutted and looked heavenward, then took the tray from Polly. 'She's a greedy one for a lady of her standing, she definitely eats enough for two!'

Polly's eyes widened. 'Hey, you don't suppose she's up the spout, do you?'

Cook glanced at Archie. 'Keep your voice down, Poll, you don't want to get fired, do you?'

She shook her head and then spoke in a hushed whisper so that Archie had to strain to hear what was being said. 'Well, we all know the shenanigans going on between her and the master and her only widowed this past six months!'

Cook's eyes widened. 'We know no such thing!' she said gruffly. 'Go and wash your mouth out with a bar of lye soap, Polly! I'd be careful what you're saying if I were you!'

Archie wondered what they were talking about. Was it a crime to devour Cook's fondant fancies? And what did his uncle have to do with it all? It was a mystery to him.

'But Cook,' Polly protested. 'You haven't seen what I've seen nor heard what I have when I've been tending to the fire in the drawing-room...' she explained. 'They forget I'm there on my hands and knees. I'm sure they think us servants must be deaf or something. Just this morning the master was arranging a secret assignation with the woman...'

Archie's ears pricked up. 'What's a secret *assugnayshun*?' he asked.

'Never you mind,' Cook said, tapping the side of her nose with her index finger, 'we'll tell you when you're twenty-one!'

What was all this with Cook saying she'd tell him certain things when he was older? It didn't make any kind of sense to him. Adults were so strange sometimes.

As if Polly realised she had spoken out of turn in front of him, she took the tray off Cook and to the sink, then proceeded to wash up the cups and plates, humming a tuneless song.

'What time will your uncle be here tomorrow to sort out those chimneys?' Cook shouted across the kitchen.

'He'll be here at first light to make an early start,' Polly replied.

'Well, if that's the case when you've finished there go and get those dust sheets out of the attic and cover all the best furniture. You can also pack some stuff away into tea chests. We can't risk ruining things. I remember when I first worked here no one thought to do any of that and the best cream chaise lounge was completely ruined. Oh, the mistress was ever so upset!'

Polly nodded. 'Don't worry, I know the drill by now. I'll sort it all out.' She neatly stacked the wet dishes and began to dry them with a tea towel. 'Archie, you can help me if you like?'

He nodded, glad of something to do.

Cook looked at him as she sliced some apples into a bowl. 'You know the master has a tutor lined up for you?'

He shook his head, that he didn't know. 'When, today?'

'No, not today, in a day or so. His name is Mr Sowerby. Don't worry, lad. He's a good tutor by all accounts. It will give you something to do as the days are long here. Can you read?'

He nodded. 'Yes, I love reading!' His eyes lit up as he spoke at the mere thought of it.

'Well, I'll see if I can find some suitable books for you then.'

He thanked Cook and followed Polly out of the kitchen.

''Ere, Archie. Don't go telling yer uncle you been helping us in the kitchen, will you? You shouldn't really as you're a gentleman of fine breeding!'

He shook his head. A gentleman indeed! He loved being with Cook and Polly in the kitchen though. Perhaps he was going to like it here after all, even if his uncle was an old grump who liked going on secret *assugnayshuns*!

***

Archie's gaze travelled from the landing window down onto the cobbled courtyard below. A horse and cart had just drawn up and Simpkins was shuffling out there to meet with it. There was a tarpaulin covering the back of the cart. On the front sat a man and young boy whose faces were black, only the whites of their eyes were showing, and their clothing so covered by soot, he couldn't even tell what colour they were supposed to be! The sweeps weren't grimy from a bit of dirt, this was something he remembered Cook and Polly speaking of yesterday. They were chimney sweeps. He watched as the man helped the boy from the cart then spoke to Simpkins about something. Cor blimey, that young boy—he was a right nipper and all! Archie realised he was probably younger than himself. He stood there transfixed as the boy leaned forward resting his hands on his knees as his body seemed to convulse. He was coughing! Did he have a cold? But no, the man seemed somewhat annoyed. He dragged him by the collar of his jacket and pointed to the back of the cart.

He was shaking him, but Archie couldn't hear what was being said as the young lad had his head down all the while.

'What are you looking at, Archie?' Cook's booming voice startled him. He swallowed, wondering whether he ought to say something.

She came up behind him and peered over the top of her gold-rimmed specs. 'That's Mr Brackley, Polly's uncle. He's a rum sort and make no mistake. But you don't need to fear him as you won't have to have anything to do with him whilst he's here.' She patted the top of his head.

'What about the boy? Is it true he has to climb right up those chimneys?'

'Fraid so.' She tutted and shook her head. 'Can't say as I like it meself. There's some new law coming into force against climbing lads being shoved up chimneys again soon, and that's all well and good, but meanwhile, it goes on and that's despite several Acts against it being passed by Parliament over the years! But I'm not the one who has arranged this, your Uncle Walter has. Well, his housekeeper, Mrs Linley, to be precise. Be it on their own consciences!'

But surely if Uncle Water knew that such a thing was happening, he'd put a stop to it?

Archie had only met Mrs Linley briefly the night he arrived at the house and he wondered about her. 'What's she like, the housekeeper?'

Cook frowned. 'Can't say as I like her much myself, we tend to keep out of one another's way. I have my domain and she has her's and never the twain shall meet!'

Domain? What did that mean?

Noticing his puzzlement, Cook said, 'It means I'm in charge of the kitchen and she's in charge of the rest of the house!'

He smiled. 'And Polly?'

'Polly does as she's bleeding well told!' She threw back her head and laughed and so did Archie, till he looked out the window again and saw Mr Brackley prodding the boy in his back. He was about to mention it to Cook, but when he turned around, she was no longer there.

***

Archie kept a low profile the rest of the morning whilst the chimneys were being swept. Much to his relief, Polly had insisted on taking him on a tour of the grounds. It was a lovely day with azure blue skies and the sun reminded him of a bright yellow egg yolk. He shielded his eyes from its powerful rays as she spoke, 'And that's about it, my lad, you've seen the flower beds, the woods and the lake.'

'What's through the door behind you?'

She turned her attention to where there was a wooden door in a tall brick wall. 'Nothing for you to concern yourself about, Archie. The door is always kept locked. Let's go this way instead and see the garden tended to by Mr Featherstone, the gardener. He grows all sorts here: runner beans, peas, potatoes, carrots, onions, herbs. You name it and he grows it. He's got a nice greenhouse you can visit as well.'

They visited the garden but there was no sign of Mr Featherstone. 'Don't look so downcast, Archie, we'll go back to the house and I bet if we ask nicely, Cook will give you one of her scones with lashings of jam and cream.' His mouth watered at the mere thought of it.

'Polly…' he began, not quite knowing how to put it. 'Your uncle…'

'Yes?' she angled her head curiously at him.

'He has a young lad with him who works up the chimney?'

She blinked several times. 'Yes, what of it?'

'I shouldn't much like to do something like that. I'd be ever so frightened if it was me.'

'Aw, so would I and all but my uncle says they get used to it and it's better than them being in the workhouse. He gives them a roof over their heads and a bed to sleep in…'

He had to admit he'd never thought of it that way before. Maybe he'd been mistaken when he thought Mr Brackley was being nasty to the boy. He couldn't be all bad if he was helping him, could he?

All thoughts of chimneys and sweeps went right out of his head when he arrived back at the kitchen with Polly. Cook made a big fuss over him and settled him down at the pine table, then placed a plate of scones in front of him and two glass pots, one containing jam and the other cream. He'd hardly ever got to eat cream in his life before except when his mother took him to visit Uncle Herbert and Auntie Marge.

He startled as Polly quickly removed his cap. 'Aye lad, you've got a lot to learn you have an' all!'

He blinked several times not understanding what he'd done but apologised anyhow.

'We'll say no more about it, Archie,' Cook reprimanded 'but when you eat at my table in my kitchen with the rest of us, you must remove your cap. And I hope to goodness you never do that when you dine with your uncle? After me complimenting you on your manners the other day and all!'

He shook his head. 'Sorry, Cook, Sorry, Polly.'

Cook smiled. 'I expect the thought of those scones stopped you thinking straight?'

He nodded, wishing they'd stop talking so he could get stuck into one.

Cook sniffed loudly. 'Polly, fetch the teapot! I wet the tea leaves a couple of minutes ago, we don't want it going stewed.'

Polly obliged as she brought the large brown earthenware pot to the table and placed it down beside three china cups and saucers.

He was about to grab at one of the scones when Polly, who had just seated herself shook her head and rolled her eyes. 'Heaven forbid, hasn't anyone taught you any manners, lad? We're going to say grace first. Cook always does that.'

'For once,' said Cook, 'I'm not going to.' Polly looked at her in amazement. 'Archie is...'

Oh dear, he didn't know what to say, he'd never been asked to say grace before. His mother'd always said a little prayer before their meals at home yet he couldn't think now exactly what she said as she seemed to change it every time. Then he remembered what they always sang at school before lunch. As he was carefully watched by the two of them he said the words, 'Thank you for the food we eat, thank you for the world so sweet, thank you for the birds that sing, thank you Lord for everything. Amen!'

Polly and Cook smiled at one another. 'Well done, Archie!' Cook said proudly, 'now you may tuck in.'

'Hang on a mo,' Polly said, 'did you wash your hands like I told you?' She stared at Archie as his face flushed bright red.

'Er no…I forgot.'

'Then over to the sink with you,' Cook said, winking at Polly, 'and scrub those mitts until they're gleaming. We'll wait for you. Meanwhile, Polly, you can be Mother and pour for us!'

He washed his hands as quickly as possible, reseating himself at the table to find one of the scones had already been placed on his plate, sliced in two and slathered in lashings of jam and cream just like Polly had told him it would. It did taste good and all. He closed his eyes as he savoured the first few mouthfuls. They were every bit as good as Ginny's cakes and the way Cook and Polly were mothering him, made it easier to be parted from the woman, but he knew he'd never forget her.

'I've managed to find some books for you, Archie,' Cook announced.

His ears pricked up. 'Really?'

'Yes, really, they were your Uncle Walter's when he was a boy. I found them in an old trunk in the attic. I've asked permission and he says you can borrow them as long as you look after them. I think you'll enjoy them as one is Robinson Crusoe and the other is Oliver Twist. I hadn't heard of any of the others but they've all got such beautiful illustrations inside of them.'

'Thank you, Mrs Stockley.' He could never imagine his uncle as a child reading such books or even playing and having fun. He couldn't even imagine him playing with any other children either. Thoughts of the man caused him to ask, 'Where is my uncle today, Mrs Stockley?'

'Your uncle is on business in London for a couple of days, so you can dine with me and Polly in the kitchen tonight if you like? Or would you rather dine on your own in the dining room?'

The thought of him being in that dark, imposing room sat by himself at that overly large table with just a candelabra for company, made him shiver. 'Oh, I'm quite happy to eat with you both,' he said quickly, causing both women to chuckle.

'It's alright,' Polly smiled. 'We thought you'd say that. You're not used to the high life as yet, but you mark my words, you're going to be a gentleman someday and you'll no longer want to dine with the likes of us.'

'Never!' he said, meaning it at the time.

***

Later that day he was introduced to his tutor, Mr Sowerby, by Polly in what he was told was 'the School Room'.

Mr Sowerby stood with his back to him as he gazed through a large arched window that overlooked the lawns and fountain below. Archie trembled as he noticed a thin wooden cane in the man's hand which he swished from side to side. His eyes pleaded with Polly for her to stay but she just winked at him.

Then the man turned and stared at him as Archie gulped. 'Dratted fly!' his new teacher exclaimed. 'It's been buzzing around the school room since I got here. I tried to swoosh it out of the way but will it go? No. I've just opened the window and hopefully, it will fly out, I don't like killing them…' he smiled. 'I'm your new teacher, Mr Sowerby, so I'm guessing you must be young Archibald?'

Archie smiled. 'Yes, sir. But I prefer to be called, Archie!'

'Very well,' Mr Sowerby smiled. 'I like someone who speaks his mind. Take a seat, young man, for I'm about to teach you your first lesson. How do you like history?'

'I like it very much, sir.' In truth, he'd hardly been taught any history at school as the classes were so large. There were supposedly fifty children in his class at school, all boys as there was a boys' section and a girls' one. But the place was so rowdy most of the time and the cane employed to deal with those ruffians who tried to run amok. It disturbed interesting lessons which he found most annoying.

'First things first then,' Mr Sowerby said, as he sat behind a large oak desk and Archie took a seat behind a matching smaller desk directly in front of him. 'Can you read and write?'

Archie nodded eagerly. 'I can, yes, sir.'

Mr Sowerby smiled. 'Splendid! Then I am sure we are going to get along nicely. I am going to read to you all about the Battle of Trafalgar and then I'm going to ask you some questions. How does that sound to you?'

He realised he was going to find lessons most interesting. 'I'd like that very much, sir.' For once he was going to have a lesson where he could hear the teacher's voice throughout and where there'd be no disruption whatsoever.

***

Archie was just leaving the schoolroom to find Polly and wondering what he'd have to do next when a hand grabbed hold of him.

He turned to see it was Polly's uncle, Mr Brackley stood there, his face blackened and what teeth he had in his head, shone through in various shades of black, green and offwhite. 'You lad, who are you? I ain't seen you 'ere before?'

'I've come here to live with my uncle, sir.'

'Have you now? Well, you look like a fit looking young specimen to me. Could you do me a favour?'

Archie recoiled from the man's fetid breath but found himself nodding, though he didn't want to do so but he was afraid to do anything else.

Brackley looked right and left along the corridor as if to check out no one else could overhear what he was about to say. 'You see, I sent me apprentice up the chimney in the drawing-room about a half hour ago and he hasn't come back. Now if he doesn't show up soon, I shall 'ave to send out a search party for him!' He chuckled. 'Of course, I can't do that, can I? As everyone else is too big to get up that chimney, but you, you're scrawny enough...so what I want you to do is follow him up there and when you find him stick this pin in his foot!' He held up a shiny long pin with a little pearl on the end of it that reminded him of the sort he'd seen ladies put in their hats to keep them in place.

Archie was horrified. He genuinely thought the first thing the man would do was save the young lad not inflict pain. 'B…but…'

Archie heard footsteps and was relieved to see Cook heading his way with a pile of clean tablecloths and tea towels in her arms. 'What's going on here, Archie?' she asked, her bottom lip jutting out. She looked furious.

He was too scared to complain about the sweep in his presence, so didn't answer.

'I was just teasing the boy,' Mr Brackley said. 'My young sweep hasn't come out of that chimney yet.' He pointed to the drawing-room.

Cook furrowed her brow. 'Well, if my memory serves me correct that chimney connects with another that comes out in the dining room, I'd check in there. I'll show you now…' She marched off with the sweep, as Archie trailed behind them. Archie was so concerned about the young lad, he wanted to check all was well.

But he hadn't banked on the scene before him when he entered, there was the young lad collapsed in a heap on the floor coughing and spluttering, a sooty mess surrounding him, the carpet saved by the presence of a large dust sheet. But it wasn't the carpet Archie was worried about—it was the boy himself.

'What have you been up to, you young rascal!' Mr Brackley shouted and brought his arm up above his own head as if about to strike the lad.

'Don't you dare!' shouted Mrs Stockley as she passed the pile of clean laundry to Archie and stepped between the sweep and his apprentice. She put up a hand in front of Mr Brackley's face, at least she wasn't scared of him. 'I won't have you hitting a young lad. You shouldn't be shoving him up chimneys, anyhow.'

'Madam,' Mr Brackley said, 'this is no business of yours.'

'Oh indeed, it is!' she wagged a finger at the man. 'Now I think you had better take that lad home and put him to bed. He's exhausted.'

Then the sweep's features softened as he seemed to have a change of heart as he said in a softer tone, 'Maybe you're right, ma'am. It has been a long day for him.' Then when Cook attended to the lad, the sweep looked at Archie and seemed to be sizing him up as he muttered under his breath. 'Need some fresh meat.'

What on earth did he mean by that? He wanted Cook to roast a fresh piece of meat for him?

'Come along,' Cook said to the boy, 'Come into the kitchen with me and I'll get you something to eat and drink, then you can go home.' She turned to Archie, 'Help me take him through to the kitchen, will you? And I'll have that laundry back off you in case you drop it.'

Archie nodded and handed the freshly laundered pile to her. He watched the sweep packing away his long brushes and sacks of soot and he wondered about him.

Chapter Four

When the boy, who he discovered was called, Bobby, had left with the sweep, Cook looked at Archie. 'What was that man saying to you earlier? You can tell me.'

Archie hesitated then swallowed. 'He wanted me to go up the chimney and stick a hat pin in the boy's foot to get him moving faster, Mrs Stockley!' Archie explained.

Cook pursed her lips. 'I knew that man was up to no good!'

Archie nodded. 'It looked as if he'd been stuck in that chimney to me.'

Cook placed both hands on her hips. 'You might well be right there. It's happened before and it doesn't bear thinking about. One time, one young lad went missing up a chimney at a big house like this and another was sent to find him to help get him out and then…' As if realising maybe she'd said too much and didn't want to frighten Archie, she let her words trail off and skillfully changed the subject. 'Then of course that's rare. Right, better get on with things. So much to do and so little time…'

There were so many questions he wanted to ask but didn't like to as Cook turned away and started putting a roast in the oven. She was quite busy this evening by the look of it. 'It's a turkey for when the master returns tomorrow. I like to get it cooked out of the way the night before and warm it up in the juices the following day,' she explained.

So maybe he'd never discover what happened to those two lads up that chimney and in a sense he was scared to ask anyhow, but he was really concerned about young Bobby. Maybe Polly might know.

He took the opportunity later when he was seated around the table with her and Cook. The fayre was simple, just a large slice of cooked ham, lettuce, tomatoes and cucumber from Mr Featherstone's garden, a wedge of cheese and a slice of crusty bread slathered in best butter. Then for pud, Cook had made an apple crumble with a thick yellow custard.

As he tucked into the crumble, he looked at Polly who frowned at him.

'Archie, you've been staring at me on and off for ages this evening. Now out with it, what's up?' she asked.

'Do you know what happened to young Bobby who was helping your uncle earlier today?'

'I heard from Cook that he got lost up the chimney, if that's what you mean?'

'I know that but what I mean is, where will he be taken to now?'

'To my uncle's home, I should think. I've already told you he's the benevolent sort, feeds the lads, clothes them and gives them shelter.' She smiled as if she was quite proud of the man.

'Them?' Cook blinked.

'Yes, there have been several in his employ. He's a good sort providing destitute boys with jobs and a roof over their heads.'

'But where are they all now? I only saw the one boy,' Archie said.

Polly let out a long breath. 'Look, he takes them on and then has to let them go when they can no longer fit up the chimney. At least they get work for a time, better than the workhouse or walking the streets begging for a crust of bread.'

'That may be so,' Cook frowned, 'and you're right as otherwise they'd become wards of the parish but when they're of no further use to your uncle, what then?'

Polly lifted her chin in a haughty fashion as if no one ought to dare ask her such an impertinent question. 'If you must know and I don't see how it is any of your business, Mrs Stockley, he has friends who can take them on. One has a market stall, the other is a pub landlord. So I expect they help elsewhere. Now is there any custard left?' She looked at Archie who felt the blood rush to his cheeks, he hadn't realised that Polly hadn't poured any custard over her crumble yet.

'It's all right,' Cook said acerbically, kicking her chair out of the way as she rose, so it scraped the flagstone floor, 'there's some left in the saucepan.'

Polly and Cook spoke no more about it and the rest of the meal was eaten in silence. Archie could sense the tension between them. Finally, Cook left the table to sit near the fire as she was prone to do of an evening in her rocking chair, whilst Polly started on the washing up, but there was so much clattering and banging about coming from the girl that it set Archie's nerves on edge.

'She's annoyed with me,' Cook whispered to Archie.

'But why?'

'Because I questioned her about those lads. She thinks the sun shines out of her uncle's backside, but I know differently.' She tapped the side of her nose with her index finger. 'I was hoping we'd be rid of him after today, but I've been informed by Simpkins he'll be back first thing in the morning.'

Archie gasped. 'Poor Bobby,' he said, sadly shaking his head.

'Yes, poor Bobby indeed,' Cook agreed.

***

From his bedroom window, Archie could see a man down below in the gardens pushing a wheelbarrow. He wore a flat cap on his head, a brown leather waistcoat over a cream shirt and dark brown trousers, tied with string around each knee. He had to be Mr Featherstone, surely? The man looked up and waved at him. Archie returned the wave. How he'd love to see that garden and what was behind that wall with the door. There was no use dwelling on things, for now, he was going to have to be content with doing the homework his new teacher had set him, and then later, he'd read the first chapter of Robinson Crusoe before going to sleep.

He must have drifted into a deep slumber as he woke in darkness with the book on his chest, he'd been that tired he hadn't even got himself ready for bed, but he was on top of the counterpane instead. There was a draught blowing in through his bedroom window as the curtains billowed in the breeze, and it looked most eerie. Cook had said there was a storm a brewing. So he carefully closed the leaded sash window and went to draw the curtains when he thought he saw a figure down below looking up at the house. Heavy rain had started to fall, blurring the window pane and when he blinked and looked again, there was no one there. Thinking he must have imagined the whole thing, he climbed into bed and shot under the covers drawing them up over his head, feeling spooked out by it all. That Mr Brackley scared him to death. What if it was him? But maybe it was Mr Featherstone instead.

He slept fitfully, dreaming of being trapped inside a sooty chimney breast with young Bobby, they were both coughing their guts up as it grew like a furnace around them and began to sear their skin. He woke with a start and then he screamed out to see the doorknob turn a fraction. His heart beat wildly as he prepared for the worse, but it was only Cook's face he saw popping around the door. She wore her hair long and loose on her shoulders and a frilled cotton cap on top of it, in her hand, she held a candle on a saucer. 'You all right, Archie?' She asked as she stepped inside. 'I heard you scream out?' The flickering candle gave her face a strange ethereal glow as if she was some sort of spectre who had appeared to check him out.

'I'm all right now,' he said, satisfied he must have imagined the earlier incident.

'Good boy. Well you get off to sleep now, I'm only next door if you need me.'

There were so many rooms in the house, he hadn't even realised she was his neighbour next door, just like Ginny, he thought as he drifted off to sleep.

The following morning, the storm had subsided and he was back in the kitchen with Cook who placed two boiled eggs in front of him and a couple of rounds of toast. At home, he was lucky to get an egg now and again, but two! This was something else.

'Are these both for me, Mrs Stockley?' He asked wide-eyed, hoping in reality they were.

'Of course, Archie. I'd hardly dish up one for myself as well on your plate now, would I?' She winked at him. 'I figured you need some feeding up. By the way, I've received instructions you're to dine with your uncle again this evening.'

He swallowed. He hadn't much enjoyed the last experience. His uncle had barely spoken a word to him and had blocked him from view as he'd leafed through his broadsheet newspaper again which had made Archie feel very unimportant and more isolated than ever.

Cook placed both hands on her hips. 'What's the matter? Most young boys of your age would be pleased to dine in style with a wealthy uncle.'

Well, he wasn't most boys. 'I don't know what to say to him, he makes me feel a bit uncomfortable.'

She smiled as she sawed through the cob loaf she had in front of her and put the round on a plate with a few others ready to toast on the long toasting fork in front of the fire. 'Aw don't go taking it to heart, it's just his way that's all. He's not a man of many words particularly when it comes to children. He doesn't know how to relate to them, see.'

'Do you think I could teach him then?' Archie perked up.

'Perhaps you could and all. I don't see why not!' Cook's eyes sparkled with good humour.

Feeling better, he began to tuck into his breakfast, cutting off the top of one of his eggs. He hesitated before applying a little salt from the cellar.

'Is there anything else troubling you?'

He turned to face Cook. 'I was wondering if that chimney sweep came back this morning? I was hoping to see Bobby to check he's all right.'

'Aye, me and all, but no sign so far.' Cook shook her head and mumbled something under her breath which Archie failed to catch, and before he could ask what she said, Polly burst into the kitchen waving her arms and yelling for help.

'Hang on, where's the fire?' Cook demanded to know.

'It's Mr Featherstone, Cook. He's had a nasty fall and I don't know what to do.'

Cook set down the loaf of bread on the counter. 'Where is he?'

'He's in the orchard, he was pruning one of the apple trees and took a nasty tumble. Good job I was there.'

Cook narrowed her eyes. 'And what were you doing there in the first place, might I ask?'

Polly's face reddened. 'I…I was going to see if I could cadge some apples for you to make us one of your lovely pies.'

'A likely story!' Cook raised her voice. 'We only had apple crumble yesterday. You've been spooning with some lad, haven't you?'

Polly began to look flustered. 'I…I have done no such thing!' she threw up the bottom of her apron in temper.

'Well whatever your explanation is, it can wait. My main concern is Mr Featherstone.' She turned to Archie, 'Lad, go and find Mr Simpkins and explain what's happened. We need his help!'

Archie nodded, not having the faintest idea where the man was, he hadn't seen him since the night he'd last dined with his uncle. He watched as in a frantic fuss, Cook and Polly left at the kitchen back door. He shoved a piece of toast in his pocket for later, then looked up and down the corridor outside. 'Mr Simpkins!' he called, his voice echoing off the corridor walls. 'Mr Simpkins!'

There was a bumping noise and a shuffling sound, then the elderly man emerged from a small room just off the reception area, yawning and stretching his arms above his head. It was obvious to Archie he'd been fast asleep as his hair looked slightly tousled, not smooth and sleek as it usually was, and he guessed that maybe the man wouldn't have much to do when his uncle wasn't at home so he napped whenever he could.

'What's the matter?' he asked.

'The gardener has fallen from a tree in the orchard and needs help, Polly and Cook are on their way there. Cook told me to ask you to help.'

The butler shook his head as if he had little sympathy for Mr Featherstone. 'He's been warned on more than one occasion to take it easy at his age. But will he listen, no? I better go and see what I can do to help. Can you wait here as I'm awaiting the imminent arrival of the sweep and his apprentice at any given moment?'

Horror struck by the butler's words, Archie found himself nodding in agreement when in reality the last thing he wanted to do was to be faced with that man again. He made his tummy turn over and the palms of his hands moist with fear. He was quite sure he wasn't the benevolent gent that Polly made him out to be. His instincts told him so. He had looked at him as if he was about to gobble him up down his belly, just like the wolf in Little Red Riding Hood. The man made his flesh crawl.

Archie watched the butler slowly shuffle away. At this rate, he'd be lucky to get to the orchard by Tuesday! And today was a Friday.

Twenty minutes later and the rescue party still hadn't returned to the house. The loud ticking of the walnut encased grandfather clock in the hallway seemed to emphasise the fact that time was passing and something was about to happen. But what?

Suddenly, Archie heard the front doorbell ring. What was he to do now? Mr Simpkins had told him to wait for the sweep. He took his time walking to the door in the hope the butler would return to answer it. But no such luck as the bell rang a second time.

As he opened the inner door, his heart flipped over and he hesitated with his hand on the doorknob. His palms felt slick with perspiration and his breaths were faster than usual. It felt as if his heart was about to pound right out of his chest, yet, he knew he had to answer the caller.

The bell rang a third time.

Slowly, he opened the door as he held his breath as if it would somehow ward off evil.

There in front of him in his grubby garb was Mr Brackley, but he was all alone, there was no boy with him. Archie looked past the man to see if he could see Bobby, but there was no sign.

'Yer took your time, didn't you?' he growled, the whites of his eyes on show. 'I've just been to another house to collect my earnings and now I'm finishing off there. I need to do another hour's work 'ere and that's me done for the week!' He slapped the palm of his hands together in satisfaction.

Archie stepped aside to allow the man access. 'Where is everyone?' he asked, as he walked into the hallway.

'The butler has had to go to the orchard,' Archie explained. He didn't intend telling him he was all alone in the house. Mrs Stockley had explained to him that once this house had a lot of staff but financial problems had caused the master to downsize to a small team of staff.

''Orright for some, he should have taken me with him, could do with scrumping a few apples!' he glowered. Then he stared at Archie again as though sizing him up. 'Yer a nice nimble lad, looks strong an' all…'

Just as Archie was about to make an excuse and leave, Cook marched into the hallway, once she saw the sweep her breezy attitude changed. 'What's happened to the lad from yesterday? I hope you haven't sent him up the chimney again!'

The sweep shook his head and laughed. 'Madam, you can be certain I'm looking after him. He's resting today. I left him at home in bed.'

Cook narrowed her eyes as if she didn't believe a word of it. 'Well, there's one chimney left to sweep in the library. How are you going to manage without the boy?'

'I've brought some extra long brushes with me, they're on the cart. Now about payment…'

'You'll have to take that up with the master, he won't be back until tonight,' Cook said sharply. She obviously didn't suffer fools gladly and Archie was so glad of that. There was no messing with Cook. No pulling the wool over her eyes and Mr Brackley could tell that much by her manner.

***

That evening, Polly informed Archie he was to wear his best bib and tucker. What on earth was that? He frowned.

'It's all right, lad, I'm only telling you to wear the same shirt and breeches as the last time you dined with your uncle.'

He would have heaved a sigh of relief except he didn't much care for that outfit at all, the ruffled shirt made him look like a girl and the collar made him itch, but he did realise he couldn't wear anything too scruffy or casual. He wasn't daft and he did aim to please his uncle. If Cook said Uncle Walter wasn't so bad then he needed to believe it as he trusted the woman entirely.

'Now,' Polly said, as she combed his hair into place. 'Mrs Linley will be back on duty here this evening. So be on your best behaviour, she won't take any messing around that's for sure!'

He nodded, he hadn't intended on messing around anyhow. 'Where has she been then?'

'None of your business!' Polly said primly, then looking at him as she caught his baffled expression, said in a softer tone, 'She's been to visit an aunt of hers who is poorly. But don't think that will soften the old biddy up, she's a tartar that one!'

He trembled. There weren't many people he was truly scared of but Mr Brackley was one, and now it seemed Mrs Linley would be another.

'For heaven's sake!' said Polly, 'don't go looking so scared, Archie. It will be all right, I'm just warning you to mind your Ps and Qs with her, that's all.'

He furrowed his brow. He knew what the letter "P" from the alphabet was and he knew what the letter "Q" was, but what did Polly mean? As if reading his thoughts, she chuckled saying, 'I just mean to mind your manners and don't go cussing any.'

As if? His mother would have boxed his ears if he cussed.

She led him to the dining room where this time his uncle was not in attendance, yet the table was set for two. He took his seat and then glanced at Polly with apprehension.

'I've been informed by Mr Simpkins that your uncle will be here shortly. Now when he comes into the room, you are to stand as a sign of respect, understood?'

'Yes, Polly.'

'Good. And don't go sitting down straight away neither, wait until he tells you to.' She wagged a finger at him.

'Yes, Polly.'

'Oh and don't go eating until after he starts eating…'

'Yes, Polly.' He stifled a yawn. There were so many rules and regulations in this house it was hard to keep up with them all. To him, it was a house that held secrets within its walls. He could hardly imagine his mother living here as a young woman. There were no portraits of her on the wall and no sign of any old toys like there was for Uncle Walter. To think that she would have once dined in this very same room, possibly eaten her dinner from the same highly polished table. She would have known Cook for sure, as Cook had been here forever and Mr Featherstone, too.

'Sit down, Archie,' Polly commanded. 'Now just remember all I told you and you won't go far wrong!' She winked at him and then turned and left the room.

Silence. A very long silence. All he could hear were the flames crackling in the hearth and the wind howling outside as darkness fell. It made the hairs on the back of his neck prickle with fear. He watched the hands of the gold carriage clock on the mantelpiece move ever so slowly. He tried to think of things to keep himself amused.

How many paintings are there on the wall? One, two, three, four, five...oh, hang on, there are two miniature paintings either side of the fireplace...

As he tried to think of something else, the main doors opened and his uncle stepped inside. Archie remembered what Polly had told him and immediately he was on his feet standing behind his chair.

'Archie,' his uncle said.

'Good evening, sir,' Archie replied, quite surprised his uncle had addressed him.

'How are those studies with your tutor coming along?'

'Very well, sir. I'm enjoying reading about all the...'

But he realised he'd lost his uncle's attention as he interrupted him with, 'I'm famished. I haven't eaten since midday!' He rubbed the palms of his hands together as if in expectation of what was to come. 'I've been travelling back from London, you see. We stopped off at a coaching inn on the way but the repast was dire, so we left shortly afterwards. I hope Cook has come up with something good this evening!'

What did he mean by "repast"? He'd ask his tutor tomorrow, must be something to do with food. His uncle could be so posh sometimes. Archie said no more as Cook entered the room carrying a big silver salver covered with a matching lid. It was so big he could only see her eyes over the top of it.

'It's your favourite, Mr Brooking!' she announced proudly as she set it down in front of him. Her cheeks were ruddied red like the breast of a robin. She always spoke fondly of his uncle but Archie could never understand why. What was so nice about the man? He couldn't for the life of him see what it might be.

For the first time ever, Archie noticed that his uncle's eyes twinkled and he actually smiled! 'Let me guess…is it smoked mackerel with new potatoes and salad?' She shook her head.

'Then it has to be steak and kidney pud with mashed potatoes, peas and your famous gravy, Mrs Stockley!'

Cook smiled coquettishly like a young lass who was being chatted up by a lad. He certainly knew how to flatter the ladies that uncle of his.

'Yes!' she announced as she whipped off the lid. Archie's stomach growled. The pie pastry looked flaky, puffed and golden and the aroma was to die for. He could see how it was his uncle's favourite as steam arose from it and he sniffed in its essence.

'Thank you, Mrs Stockley. I shall enjoy this!'

Archie frowned. Wasn't he allowed any pie then?

Seeing his face, Cook said, 'It's all right, Archie, I've got something else for you. Polly's just bringing it in.'

Archie turned to see Polly carrying a small tray with a bowl of something steamy on it. She set it down before him. 'Beef broth and lentils', she said. Then whispered in his ear, 'Cook thought steak and kidney pie would be too heavy on your stomach going to bed…'

He watched both women leave the room. Then closed his eyes as his uncle muttered a prayer of thanks for the meal they were about to eat. But before he even picked up his knife and fork, he said to Archie. 'You know when I was your age I loved steak and kidney pud, would you like some?'

Archie nodded. Then remembering his manners, said, 'Yes, please, Uncle Walter.'

Walter smiled broadly and it was as if some sort of iceberg had melted between them. He picked up a small empty dinner plate beside him and sliced off a small piece of his pie handing it to Archie. After that there were no stopping him as he told Archie all about what life was like at the house when he was young, but never once did he mention Archie's mother. Yet, his eyes came to life as he spoke about his old governess, Kitty Periwinkle, who had taught him to read, and tales of how Mr Featherstone had started off at the house as a help to the old gardener and had gradually taken on his position.

Oh, what fun he'd had, camping in the woods with friends in the summer, fishing in the lake and sitting out in the grounds at night, star gazing. Indeed it sounded to Archie as if his uncle had enjoyed a very charmed childhood. He longed to ask about his mother. Had she gone star gazing too? But for some reason, he decided not to. He didn't know his uncle well enough as yet. He was just going to have to bide his time.

There was a knock at the dining room door as they were tucking into their dessert. Cook had made them lemon meringue and Archie had never tasted it before. The yellow part was sharp but sweet at the same time, tickling his taste buds and the meringue was soft and swirly like clouds in the sky. He really liked it.

He watched as Mrs Linley entered the dining room with a stern expression on her face. She didn't look as old as Cook, but much older than Polly. Her hair was tightly scraped back from her face into a bun, making her expression look most severe, and her dress was as black as a coal pit edged with a white frilly collar making quite a contrast. Around her waist, she wore a set of keys which clinked as she walked towards them.

'Sir, might I speak to you about something?' She said, pausing, as she approached the table.

'Can't it wait, Mrs Linley?' His uncle's voice had a note of exasperation to it as if he didn't want to be disturbed and for once was enjoying his nephew's company.

'I'm afraid it really can't. That gentleman is by the door, the chimney sweep we arranged to call here, though he ought to be by the servant and tradesman's entrance...' she let out a breath. 'He says he hasn't been paid for his recent services. I've been absent as you know, due to unforeseen circumstances...' she let out another breath. 'So, I need to check it out.'

'Isn't Simpkins around?'

She shook her head. 'I can't seem to find him, sir.'

His uncle dropped his dessert spoon with such a clatter on his plate that it startled Archie. He was obviously in a bad mood.

'I really don't know what I'm paying that man for if he's not around!' he glowered, then he followed Mrs Linley leaving Archie all alone.

From his seat, he could hear his uncle's voice but not what he was saying. The door was slightly ajar and they weren't too far from the front door, it was just down the corridor.

Whatever his uncle was saying, he wasn't too pleased by the sound of it. Then he heard Mr Brackley shouting, 'You've not heard the last of this! You haven't paid me enough for my services! My fees have gone up!'

'I've just paid you what was previously agreed and you'll get no more!' His uncle shouted, then the door was slammed shut. Obviously, Mr Brackley had been sent away with a flea in his ear. Maybe it was a good thing, Archie thought. He never, ever, wanted to see a young boy forced to climb a chimney again.

Chapter Five

Archie traced a raindrop on the inside of the window with his fingertip. It had been raining for a couple of days and he longed to get outside. He was going to ask Mr Featherstone if he needed help in the garden. Now that he'd fallen from that tree and injured himself, the man was bound to need some assistance. He'd seen him passing with his wheelbarrow, pausing to rub his aching back. Most of all, he longed to see that garden for himself and the walled area behind it. It intrigued him, but Polly had told him she had instructions from his uncle that he was to remain indoors as the weather was particularly harsh. High winds blew across the trees, bending them out of shape. There wasn't even a bird in sight. He wondered where they were—sheltering from the storm if they had any sense he supposed. He hoped they were safe somewhere. Meanwhile, a piano tutor was sent to the house. Archie had never played a musical instrument in his life but found himself taking to lessons like a duck takes to water. Miss Greening, with her long auburn hair and sparkling hazel eyes, taught him the difference between the ivories and the black keys on the piano. He'd had lessons every day of the week alongside his normal school lessons so they kept him busy, but by the end of the week, the sun was starting to peep out through the clouds and his uncle finally gave him permission to go outside. A hurricane that had whirled through the village had ripped off the roof of the bakery and damaged some trees in its path. Luckily no one was hurt, but he guessed maybe Uncle Walter had been right to keep him indoors.

Archie waited on the steps of the house in front of the ornamental fountain for Mr Featherstone to pass by. He knew by now that he passed there several times a day and sometimes tended the nearby lawns. Today was no exception as the man came by holding a pair of shears. He looked a little pale but otherwise seemed fit enough.

'Hello, young lad,' he said, as he stopped to make small talk with Archie. 'So you must be the master's nephew?'

'I am, yes, sir. I'm Archie. I waved to you from the window the other day. Do you remember?'

'Aye, I do. I've heard all about you from Cook and Polly.'

Archie frowned. What had they been saying about him? He hoped it was all good and it wasn't that he didn't like wearing that silly frilly shirt and stiff pair of breeches or that they had to pester him to wash his hands or remove his cap before meals. But he needn't have worried as the old man's face broke out into a wide grin.

'They've only told me good things I can assure you.' He pushed back the peak of his flat cap and Archie could see how brown and weatherworn his face was but his blue eyes were crystal clear.

'I've been waiting to see you,' said Archie.

'Oh and why is that, young man?'

'I heard you had a nasty fall from one of the apple trees so I figured as how I might help you. I'm good at climbing up trees, see. I wouldn't want no paying either…'

Mr Featherstone chuckled. 'That's very kind and thoughtful of you, Archie. Happen I could do with a little help as my lumbago is playing up something rotten these days especially after that fall…'

He didn't know what on earth lumbago was but he took the gardener's word for it. 'So, please can I help you, Mr Featherstone?'

The gardener rubbed his chin. 'I don't see why not, lad, but we'll have to clear it with your uncle first, then if he says yes, I shall pay you with all the apples you can eat!'

Archie smiled, he liked the sound of that.

'Archie!' a voice he recognised called from behind him. 'Luncheon is ready, hurry up! Then you have school lessons upstairs!' It was Polly's voice, sounding sharper than usual. Cook had said she was a bit tetchy as her uncle had been dismissed and not paid what he said he was owed. Apparently, he'd been putting pressure on her to get the money for him.

'Bye, young man!' Mr Featherstone said, 'Don't forget to ask your uncle for permission to help me!'

'I won't,' he said, waving goodbye, then he watched the old man walking off towards the bushes near the fountain as Polly waited impatiently on the steps with her hands on her hips like she meant business. He'd better hurry, he didn't want to get his ears boxed. To be fair to her though, although she'd threatened it often enough, it just wasn't her style. Now Mrs Linley on the other hand, she was a right tartar, he wouldn't want to get on the wrong side of her.

Waiting for him in the kitchen was a plate of fluffy creamy mashed potatoes and two thick pork sausages. His favourite. Yum.

Cook looked at him. 'Sit yourself down, lad. What were you doing talking to Mr Featherstone?'

He knew the drill by now so went across to the old stone bosh to wash his hands, carefully rolling his sleeves up to the elbow not to get them soaked. 'I was asking him if I could help in the garden.'

Cook quirked an eyebrow. 'Oh? And why would that be?'

Archie slathered his hands with the soap then rinsed them in the water. 'Because I figured he's an old man who needs a bit of help now and again.'

Cook smiled and then handed him a towel. 'Come and sit down and eat your food, you're a good lad, Archie.'

***

Archie plucked up the courage to ask his uncle whilst they dined that night if he might help Mr Featherstone in the garden.

His uncle raised an inquisitive brow. 'I hadn't had you down as being interested in gardening, Archie?' he said.

'I never had a garden see, not at Dock Street, we didn't, just a backyard.'

His uncle nodded. 'Yes, I do realise that. I have visited your house on more than one occasion as you're well aware. It's a choice in life your mother made to live like that...' he said brusquely, causing Archie to bristle with fear. It was the first time his uncle had mentioned his mother since he'd set foot in the house. What did he mean by that?

He cleared his throat. 'Sorry, sir, what do you mean?'

He thought for a moment he glimpsed compassion behind his uncle's eyes. 'I'm sorry, I shouldn't have mentioned it…' he paused for a spell as if he was having trouble finding the right words to say. 'It's just your mother had a good life here and she left it all behind. She was much loved. Anyhow, we'll speak no more of it.'

Before Archie had a chance to ask anything else, his uncle lifted the evening newspaper and thumbed his way through it. Archie wasn't daft, he was doing it to block out any difficult comments from him. When it was time to leave the table, Archie broached the subject of the garden again.

'I suppose it will be all right, Archie,' his uncle said, folding the newspaper and looking at him curiously. 'As long as you don't overdo things as you have your studies and pianoforte lessons to fit in.'

'I won't, sir. I promise.'

'Very well then, you may leave the table.'

Archie hadn't felt this happy in a long while and he was sure his uncle had smiled to himself without realising he'd noticed.

***

Early next morning, Archie found Mr Featherstone waiting for him outside with a wheelbarrow beside him. 'Your uncle has given me orders that I can work you no longer than an hour a day. So what I'd like to do is take you to the orchard and ask you to collect all the windfall apples for me. Put all the good 'uns in this wheelbarrow and I've got a large wooden crate you can drop the battered and bruised ones in. We don't keep them stored together as they can turn the

65

others. One overripe or mouldy apple can ruin all the others! We don't want to undo our good work.'

Archie nodded, wondering what happened to the bruised fruit. Back home they could feed families with all of those. The kids were ravenous, so much so that any stranger they saw toss an apple stump on the floor, they grabbed for almost before it landed on the pavement.

'Of course, what I just told you can apply to people too in life, lad.' Mr Featherstone looked him in the eye as if to drive his point home.

Archie frowned. He didn't see how a person could be compared to an apple! 'Sorry, sir. I don't understand…'

'Well it's like this, a rotten person can influence others around them. So keep away from bad people who do wicked things!'

'I think I understand,' Archie said thoughtfully. 'Can I push the wheelbarrow for you, Mr Featherstone?'

The old man nodded. 'It's heavy, mind as you go.'

'That's all right. I'll tell you if it gets too hard for me.'

The gardener patted Archie on the back. 'Do you know what, Archie. I reckon we're going to get along famously!'

They spent the next hour in the orchard, Archie was spellbound by the variety of different apples grown there, most ripe for the picking, but Mr Featherstone said they were to leave those and only collect the windfall ones. No wonder there were so many of them, Archie speculated, after the storm the other night!

He was quite sorry when he had to return to the house. Polly had been despatched to collect him as his tutor had arrived.

'Never mind, Archie, you can help me again tomorrow!' The gardener said in a kindly fashion. 'You've been a great help to me as I haven't had to keep bending over to pick up those blessed apples, so you've saved my back for me!' he chuckled.

'Thank you!' Archie beamed. 'Might I take a few with me? I'd like to ask Cook if she'll bake one of her apple crumbles, I'm sure she'll let you have some too with lashings of thick creamy custard!' He licked his lips at the mere thought of it.

'I'd like that very much,' the old man replied, as he handed Archie an armful of apples.

Polly smiled. 'The lad's right, Mr Featherstone, Cook wouldn't mind setting another place when she makes that crumble. You should join us.'

He smiled and tipped his cap to her. Then Polly and Archie turned and made their way back to the house, with Polly carrying some of the apples in her folded apron.

***

Archie was awoken that night by the sound of tapping on his window pane. What was that? In his drowsy state, as his heart thudded, he made his way over to the window in the inky darkness. He drew back one of the drapes but could see nothing outside except the trees silhouetted in the background and the silver rays of a half moon.

Tap! Tap! Tap! There it was again. He hadn't dreamt it, someone was throwing small stones against his window pane. He strained to see who it might be.

Then he noticed a female form standing below. For a moment, he thought it was his mother come to life again as joy flooded through him, but as his eyes got accustomed to the semi-darkness, he made out the outline of Polly below. He struggled to lift the sash window to see what she wanted.

As he leaned out of the window, she hissed. 'Come down, Archie. I need to speak to you!'

He nodded, curious as to why she hadn't come to his room instead and why she wanted to speak to him outside.

He quickly located his dressing gown and slippers and made his way downstairs and out through a side door which he left on the latch, so he could get back inside again.

But whilst outside he could see no sign of Polly. He didn't want to call her for fear of waking up the household, but he figured it must have been of some urgency for her to wake him up in the first place.

He scouted around the side of the house to see if there was any sign of her, the wind had started whipping up and now outside it was beginning to feel most eerie with the moon reflecting long shadows onto the ground in front of him. He heard footsteps behind himself and was about to turn when he felt a hand clamp over his mouth, dragging him back towards the trees. It was a big hand and he was finding it difficult to breathe as he struggled to release himself. This couldn't be happening to him, it was a like his worse nightmare.

'Be careful, Bill,' he heard a female voice say, and then he saw the face of who it belonged to. It was a young woman who looked very much like Polly, but it wasn't her, this lady looked a few years older. The whites of her eyes were on show as if she was horrified by what was taking place. He began to kick out to try to escape "Bill's" clutches, but the man was too strong for him and he found himself being dragged towards the bushes, his heels bumping across the rough stony ground. Then the man suddenly released his hand from his mouth, so Archie could breathe again, but now had his arm around his throat so he was held in the crook of his arm and unable to escape. He could smell the man's beery breath and disgusting body odour and it made him gag.

'Bill,' the young woman was pleading, 'we've made a mistake, let him go.'

'No way, Flora. He's coming with us!' Suddenly he swung Archie around to face him and he could see a face he recognised all too well, it was Mr Brackley the chimney sweep. Revulsion filled him as he started to shudder with fear. 'Now listen here, lad,' the man said in a slightly softer tone. 'I'm taking you with us as payment. Your uncle refused to pay up fully what I was owed. Me other lad isn't well at the moment, so I'm taking you.'

Horrified, Archie felt tears prick the back of his eyes. 'Please let me go, sir, and I won't say anything, honest, I won't!' he pleaded.

'That's not possible. I've collected you as collateral damage,' he explained. 'A gentleman always pays his debts and your uncle is obviously not one of those fine fellows! He's a welcher and you're the price he has to pay for diddlin' me out of what I was owed!'

Archie's eyes widened as he feared the man might strike him at any given moment. 'B…but where are you taking me?'

Flora draped her arm around his shoulders. 'We've got the horse and cart ready and we're taking you to the East End,' she said in a kindly fashion, almost as though she were taking him on a jolly jaunt somewhere and not kidnapping him in the middle of the night.

At least it was an area he knew, which was of small comfort to him. Maybe he'd see Ginny again. But what about Cook, Polly and Mr Featherstone? Wouldn't they wonder what had happened to him? And his uncle, although he often didn't see much of him, they were beginning to form a bond with one another. Now he had settled into the house he really didn't want to leave. But what option did he have?

Bill bundled him onto the back of the cart, warning him to stay put beneath the old tarpaulin. The woman was made to sit with him to ensure he wouldn't escape. What could he do? There was no way out for him and it made him so sad that he ended up crying himself into a fitful sleep.

Some time later he drew back the tarpaulin with his hand. Dawn was beginning to break as the sun sneaked above the rooftops, giving off a golden glow which reflected onto the puddles of water on the streets below. The horse and cart drew up outside a pub in a dirty grimy street he didn't recognise. The street was a long one with red bricked houses facing another similar looking street, and what appeared to be the odd shop peppered here and there. He had been instructed to lie low on the back of the cart with an old blanket that reeked of damp dogs and rotting vegetables, his only bit of warmth under the tarpaulin. All the while on the journey there he kept thinking this couldn't be happening to him and it was a bad dream. Maybe he'd eaten too much of Cook's apple crumble and custard last night and he'd wake up at any moment back in his own bed. But when the cartwheels stopped rumbling and he was roughly pulled off the back of the cart by a strong, rough pair of hands, he knew this was no dream, it was a bleeding nightmare.

'Now you keep quiet, you hear?' Bill Brackley commanded as he narrowed his eyes. He looked tired and unwashed.

Archie nodded. He wouldn't dare cry out for fear of being clipped across the head by that man.

'Archie,' Flora said kindly, 'this is a pub we've got digs at for time being. I've got a little pallet for you in the corner of the room to sleep on and you can have something to eat...'

Before she had a chance to finish what she was saying, Bill glared at her. 'There's no time for that!' he growled.

'But surely you can't be thinking of sending the boy up the chimney so soon, he hasn't slept much all night and he must be starving!'

'Then he'll sleep all the better for it tonight and appreciate what little grub I choose to give him. Look, I told you that I want him kept small to get plenty of work out of him. Now he'll graft all the better today to get out of that bloody chimney and back to a bowl of scraps and a place to sleep! What did you expect to give him? Fresh meat?' He laughed in a raucous fashion at his own sarcastic comment.

The words *fresh meat* sent a shiver skittering down his spine. They were the very words Bill had used the other day when he'd appeared to size him up. Back then though Archie had assumed he was talking about food, but to his horror, he now realised what the man meant! He, Archie Ledbetter, was the fresh meat! He realised with dread, this had been his plan all along. If only he'd cottoned on, he could have told Cook who'd probably have warned his uncle to take care.

Flora shook her head then glanced at Archie with a worried frown on her face. He wondered what had happened to poor Bobby, so far there had been no mention of the boy.

As they passed through the long tap room which wasn't as yet open to the public, Archie noticed a middle-aged woman behind the bar, polishing it. It smelled strongly of lemon and lavender, a scent he associated with Cook and for a fleeting moment it gave him comfort.

'So, this is your new apprentice, is it?' the woman said brightly.

Bill scowled. 'Aye, it is, ma'am, now if you don't mind, I need to get him prepared for a day's work.'

'What's the lad's name?' the woman shouted after them but Bill didn't answer and Flora looked too frightened to do so.

Archie turned and whispered, 'Archie, miss.' But she couldn't hear him but he could tell she had seen he was trying to reply to her and smiled at him.

'Maybe the lad can tell me himself some other time,' she said, in a kindly fashion.

Bill harrumphed as they left the tap room to climb some meandering stone steps that obviously led to the living quarters. 'The boy can tell her some other time!' he mocked. He grabbed hold of Archie's hand and cruelly squeezed it. 'You don't tell that woman anything, understood?'

'Be careful, Bill,' Flora scolded, 'you're hurting the lad. Then as if noticing the tears in Archie's eyes, said, 'If you want to get plenty of work out of the rascal, don't go causing any injuries, mind.' She winked at Archie when Bill wasn't looking.

Bill dropped his hand. 'Maybe you're right. Now I want a little drink before we leave for a day's work.'

He fumbled in his trouser pocket and produced a rusty key, inserting it into the lock of a brown varnished door. The lock turned and he pushed open the door. 'Home sweet home!' he declared, as Archie shivered with anticipation of what was in store for him.

Chapter Six

Archie blinked several times. So this was his new home. He gulped. A large wire-haired hound, bounded forward to greet him almost knocking him off his feet as he tried to lick Archie's face.

'Meet Duke!' Bill said, 'Don't go trying to escape neither or I'll set him on you!' Then he looked at the dog. 'Go get him, Duke!' As if on command, Duke emitted a low growl which took Archie aback. Maybe the dog wasn't as friendly as he first thought.

'In the corner, Duke!' Bill bellowed. The dog slunk away with his belly near the floor as if trying to make himself appear smaller to his master, yet he had done nothing wrong. He circled around in a corner of the room before settling himself down on a few grimy coal sacks and whimpered as if feeling sorry for himself.

What had happened there? Archie wasn't quite sure but what he did know was that he and the dog were both scared witless by Bill Brackley.

'Get me my medicine, Flora!' Bill growled and then to Archie's astonishment he slapped the young woman hard on the backside. He could tell by her expression she didn't like it at all as she gritted her teeth, then turning towards Bill pasted a smile on her face.

What kind of medication did Bill take? Was he ill? But all became clear as Flora trotted off to a cupboard and then extracted a bottle of what appeared to be rum to Archie and poured a tot into a small glass schooner, which she set down before him on the scrubbed table. He sat and drank the glass over his head, wiping his lips with the back of his hand and letting out a low rasping noise. 'More!' he demanded. So Flora poured him another tot, then another. Then she smiled and winked at Archie as Bill began to yawn and his eyes began to close as he rested his head on the table.

'Better get you to bed, Bill, or you'll be good for nothing later on. C'mon, you've had a busy night...'

He roused himself and made his way over to a curtained off area, where Archie could just make out a bed behind it. Flora helped him into bed, then left the area as she closed the curtains so Bill was out of view. Then she approached Archie and whispered, 'Right, he'll be out cold for a couple of hours due to the rum and driving overnight, so hoppit! I'll say you ran off when he wakes so's I don't get into trouble, but please don't tell anyone about me involvement in this, will yer?'

'No, I won't, ma'am,' he smiled. What a lovely woman she was setting him free like this. He could guess she wanted no part of his kidnapping to begin with but was probably bullied by Bill into going along with it.

He was just about to leave, rejoicing in his good fortune, when he heard a voice coming from the corner next to the dog. He hadn't noticed anyone else there hidden under the sacks. 'Mr Brackley!' the voice croaked, sounding quite weak, 'the new boy is leaving! Wake up!'

Archie noticed a familiar face in the corner, it was the young sweep, Bobby. He wished he'd shut up but there were the sounds of Bill stirring, the thud of his boots on the floor, then the swish of the dividing curtain as roughly he drew it back to face Archie.

'What's going on here?' he growled, as he glowered at him.

'N…nothing, Bill. Bobby's mistaken, I was just about to send the new boy out on an errand to ask the landlady for a tot of gin for meself,' said Flora.

Bill's eyes enlargened. 'Are you mad, woman? You can't let him do things like that. Young Bobby is quite right. Come here, lad…' The boy smiled, obviously glad he'd pleased his master. ''Cos you been such a good lad and can't go up chimneys at present, you can keep an eye on the new lad to make sure he don't escape. Here, have a tot o'rum, it'll warm the cockles of yer 'eart!'

Looking dubious, as Bill poured out the rum, Bobby took the proffered glass and slowly took a sip, recoiling as he tasted it. It looked as if he was about to say, 'Yuck!' but thought better of it. 'Yes, it tastes good to me, Mr Brackley.' Then he pasted a smile on his face just like Flora had done earlier on her own. It was as if they both wore masks in front of the man for fear of upsetting the apple cart. Another shiver skittered down Archie's spine as he recalled what Mr Featherstone had said about the bad apples spoiling those around them. If ever a person could be described as "a bad apple" then surely Bill Brackley was a fine example of one of those.

'Good. Drink the rest all in one go!' Bill commanded.

Swallowing and trembling, Bobby drank it as told, then dissolved into a fit of coughing. 'Now get back in the corner with Duke. You, Archie, you can have some after you've been up the chimney, later. Flora, go and get him some water and a bit of that stale bread that's left over. You're right, he can't work on an empty stomach. And don't go thinking of escaping as Duke'll have you and Bobby will be keeping watch!'

Bobby appeared to smirk at him. How could he have ever felt sorry for the boy when he was quite prepared to dob him in? He could have been well away from here by now. He would have tried to find Ginny. He could have asked directions to his old street, but now he was stuck in a small living space with a brute of a man, a telltale tit of a kid, a dubious dog and a lady who did seem to care about his welfare but would always put Bill first.

***

'What do you mean Archie is missing?' Mrs Stockley stood with hands firmly placed on her hips as she questioned Polly in the kitchen.

'I just went upstairs, Cook, to wake Archie for breakfast but there's no sign of him!'

Cook relaxed. 'Aw that'll be because he's helping Mr Featherstone in the orchard again.'

'No, I've already checked. The gardener hasn't seen him this morning.'

'What about the school room?'

'Yes, I've searched all over the house. The lad must have run away. How are we going to tell Mr Brooking?'

'Well, we're not, not until we've looked some more and don't mention this to Mrs Linley either as she'll blame us and have our guts for garters. Come on, I'll help you look. The master had his breakfast early then left the house for business in the city.

Perhaps we can find the lad before he returns this evening.'

'Just a thought…' Polly said smiling. 'Might he have taken the boy with him?'

Cook shook her head causing Polly's smile to vanish. 'No, certainly not. Why would he take Archie with him when he's got an important meeting to attend?' Sometimes Polly could be so silly, Cook thought. She was now beginning to worry about the boy herself. He seemed quite happy at the house, she could never begin to imagine him running away from here and where would he run to anyway? He had no home of his own. 'Mr Sowerberry is due soon, we'll ask him if Archie might have said something that indicated he was unhappy here, though I very much doubt it as he seemed content enough to me!'

'You're right, Cook. He did like it here and all. He loved your cooking so much and given time would have put on a bit more weight. He was looking the healthiest I'd ever seen him since arriving here.'

Cook had to agree. He did love her cooking, particularly her puddings and pies. 'I've never seen a lad enjoy his food so much and I am rather fond of him!' She wiped away a tear with the edge of her pinafore.

Polly patted Cook's shoulder to comfort her. 'Aw Cook, we'll find him. Maybe he's gone on an adventure. He was always talking to me about the woods and the garden behind the brick wall.'

Cook's heart filled with dread. 'Oh my goodness, I hope he hasn't found the grave. Maybe that's what has set him off. If he read the inscription he'd realise a lot about his Ma.'

'Let's hope he doesn't find it. I had warned Mr Featherstone not to allow him in there but I suppose he could have climbed over the wall and found it.'

Cook shook her head and looked heavenward. 'Poor Alicia, she'd never have run away if it hadn't been for…'

Polly looked at her sympathetically and touched her hand. 'Now don't go upsetting yourself, Mrs Stockley. We all know that Alicia left a fine life of luxury behind after something happened to upset her.'

'I was so fond of that young lady,' Cook sniffed. 'She didn't deserve what happened to her. To think of her struggling to survive and living a life of near poverty.'

'I know, it seems so unfair.' Polly draped a reassuring arm around Cook. 'What we have to do now is see if we can find Archie. Mind you, I don't know how we'll break it to the master if we don't.'

It didn't bear thinking about. Archie had been placed in their care and now Cook felt like as well as letting the master down, she'd also let Alicia down, too.

***

'I can't wear these, they won't fit properly!' Archie muttered in disgust.

'These are the only clothes we've got,' Flora said firmly, 'and don't let Bill hear you talking like that or you'll get a backhander.'

Archie glanced across to where Bill was fast asleep in the armchair snoring his head off. He looked a right mess in an offwhite singlet that was full of stains. 'Sorry, Flora,' he said. 'I know you're trying to help me…'

'Sssh,' she warned in a whisper, 'don't let either Bill or Bobby hear you letting on I'm on your side or I'll pay for it.'

Reluctantly, he put on the grubby tattered breeches and jacket, which had seen better days and were a tad too large. 'I suppose they'll have to do, I can't go around in my dressing gown and nightshirt.'

'And you can't go around in those bedroom slippers neither. I'll nip over to get you a pair of old boots from the dolly shop across the road. You'll need them for when he sends you up chimneys. I'll take your slippers with me to make sure I buy the correct size.'

'But I don't want to go up any chimneys,' he whined.

'I know, but I plan to get you away from here as soon as I can. For now, do as you're told, be a brave boy.'

He stifled a sob, then heard a grunt as Bill let out a loud snore. 'What time do we have to leave?'

'In one hour it will be half past nine. He's booked in to sweep a couple of chimneys in the same street. Now, I want to warn you that as well as that he'll try to get you to nab some valuables too. But he's crafty as he doesn't get the boys to take much, he gets them to take stuff that might not be missed for a while or things that he thinks people might assume they've mislaid.'

Archie didn't like the sound of that at all. 'But I'm no thief!' he protested.

Flora put the palms of her hands on his shoulders. 'I know that, Archie. But remember we 'ave to play the game for now, darlin'.' He looked into her bewitching hazel brown eyes and saw kindness there. She had a lovely face, she was much prettier than Polly, and although he had mistaken Flora for Polly in the darkness, he guessed they were unrelated as Flora appeared to be some sort of girlfriend to Bill. If she'd been brought up as a lady he guessed she'd look all soft and refined, but she had a slightly tough edge to her as if her lifestyle had knocked the stuffing out of her, and it wasn't even her fault. One thing he knew for sure was that he trusted her.

Duke had been sniffing around him and hadn't growled since so he guessed the threat of the dog going for him was a ruse by Bill, but Bobby, he didn't trust at all. He stared hard at the boy as he was sat in the corner playing with a couple of old marbles, rolling them across the bare floor.

'I know you're mad as hell at Bobby for warning Bill you were about to leave here, but believe me, I know the reason he did it is because if you do leave here, Archie, there'd be no one to take his place up the chimneys and Bill will work him hard again. You can't blame him, can you?'

That gave Archie something to think about and he guessed if he were in his rotten boots he'd feel exactly the same. What did he mean if he were in the lad's boots? He was. His heart sank at the thought of it.

Later, when Bill had sobered up over a weak cup of tea and a hunk of bread and cheese, he took Archie out to the cart. 'Now I'll tell you exactly what to do, you behave yourself and don't go telling folk I've kidnapped you else you'll get a belter from me, understood?' He raised a fist, causing Archie to step backwards in fear. He nodded tentatively.

Bill dropped his fist, then said in a softer tone, 'That's all right then. Now you can sit beside me as long as yer behave yourself.'

Bill lifted him onto the long seat at the front of the cart. One thing Archie intended doing on this journey was to watch out for any familiar landmarks to see if he recognised where he was. Maybe he could jump off the cart and run away if it slowed down at any time.

But much to his disappointment, he didn't recognise anywhere at all as the cart rattled along cobbled streets which gave way from run-down houses to more upmarket ones with pillars and flowers in the front gardens of posh terraced houses. How the other half lived! It seemed a case of the haves and have-nots to him. How on earth could his mother have left a beautiful home for the grimy street they'd lived on he'd never know and how he wished she were here right now.

***

They were allowed into the property at the tradesmen's entrance by a sparky young housemaid who seemed well organised and friendly. 'Go through,' she ordered. 'And watch you don't get any soot over the master and mistress's valuables neither.'

Archie noticed how Bill quirked a brow at that comment. He tipped his flat cap. 'Ma'am, me and the lad are clean workers and we always do a good and thorough job for our many satisfied customers.'

'He looks a bit big to be a climbing boy!' she said, taking a long hard stare at Archie. 'The last one you brought here was much smaller than him.'

'Aye, that one was his brother. Archie here is quite thin and a bit older granted, but still capable.'

She sniffed. 'Well as long as you do a good job, I don't much care. You can start in the drawing-room.'

Bill nodded, then when she was out of sight, he said, 'Go look under them dust covers Archie and tell me what you see.'

Archie guessed he'd asked him as he didn't want to get caught out himself. He did as he was told, gingerly drawing back one cover with his thumb and forefinger. 'It's some sort of glass cabinet,' he said.

'And more importantly,' said Bill, 'what happens to be inside of it?'

'Looks like some small ornaments, fancy silver snuff boxes, thimbles and such.'

'Good, we'll take a couple of things here and there. Not too much mind, I don't want to get accused of being greedy!' he chuckled.

Archie didn't see anything to laugh about. He didn't like the idea at all. He thought it odd that he was near to so much finery, yet none of it was his. But to pocket it was wrong in his eyes.

'Now then, lad,' Bill said. 'I want you to climb up that chimney there and scrape up the soot with a scraper, brush it up and push it behind you. I've brought an hanky for you to tie around yer nose and mouth and watch your eyes.' For a moment Archie thought he cared about him but then he went on to say, 'Don't want you out of action too soon, want to get my money's worth out of you. You can blame that uncle of yours for the situation you now find yerself in. If he'd paid what I was askin', you wouldn't be in such a pickle right now, would yer?'

Archie gulped. The chimney breast was quite wide and it was tall too. He clambered inside it and looked up but he couldn't see anything. It was so dark and he was scared. His teeth began to chatter as he hung the cloth bag containing the scraper and brush over his shoulder.

'Hurry up there!' Bill growled.

Gingerly, he pulled himself up by placing a foot on a brick that was jutting out. Thankfully there was one higher up on the other side too and by pushing down on his arms he got himself up inside the bottom of the chimney flue.

'Keep going, lad!' Bill bellowed. 'You don't want me to light a fire beneath to force you up, do you? I've done that a time or two to some of the slower boys!'

'Oh, no!' Archie shouted back down the flue. He thought he heard Bill chuckling as he began to scrape away at the hardened soot, then used the brush to sweep it away. Some of it flew towards his face, so he closed his eyes, but it didn't stop him coughing and spluttering from where it got into his mouth and up his nose. He adjusted the hanky so it covered them properly.

He realised he had to be careful with his eyes so he could see where he was going. No wonder Bobby hated doing this so much and he was much younger, too. It was petrifying. Archie decided the best way to deal with this was to imagine he was doing something else entirely. He pretended in his mind he was out on a sunny day climbing a tree. The sky was blue, the birds were singing and everything was all right in his world.

'Good lad!' he heard Bill shouting down below breaking into his daydream, 'you're a natural at this, keep going!'

It made him feel good that Bill was pleased with his work but he didn't want to keep doing this even though he appeared to be good at it.

Finally, after a few minutes of frantic scraping to prevent Bill from lighting that fire down below, he noticed as he edged his way up, a faint shaft of light coming to meet him as he got to the top of the chimney. A gentle breeze hit his face and breathing was a lot easier for him. He half hoped he'd be able to push himself through to the top and get out on the roof to run away, but he realised if he tried that he could get stuck. If he'd been Bobby's size he bet he could do that though.

'Are you at the top yet?' he heard Bill shouting below, but his voice sounded far away and echoing.

'Yes!' he shouted back down.

'Come down slowly then,' Bill advised. 'You won't be able to see where you're going, so take your time.'

It was a little hair raising as he lost his footing several times and feared he'd fall into the fire grate. But eventually he found himself at the bottom with his heart thumping heavily, thoroughly exhausted and holding on to the brickwork for support. He was on solid ground at last.

Bill was beaming. 'Good lad. Now there's only another five to do!' he said, slapping the palms of his hands together as Archie watched him through sooty lashes and groaned to himself.

By the time they'd finished the whole house, Archie felt like he could no longer stand, his elbows and knees felt sore and to his dismay, he noticed trickles of warm blood running down his arms and legs.

A young maid entered the kitchen where they were finishing off. 'I've brought you both some refreshments,' she said. She looked kind-hearted and had a big beaming smile which turned to a look of horror when she saw Archie's knees. While Mr Brackley was helping himself to a round of bread and butter and a slice of thick ham with a cup of tea, she turned to Archie. 'Let me clean those wounds for you.'

Archie immediately shook his head. 'Better not, I might get into trouble with Mr Brackley for it.'

'Stuff and nonsense,' she said firmly, then addressing the sweep said, 'I often clean up the little sweep's sores, can I clean his?'

Bill, who was happily filling his face just nodded and said, 'Aye, I'll be brining him in front of the fire tonight to toughen up his skin, it's his first day on the job.' Archie guessed he had to be nice in front of the maid in case she kicked up a fuss and told her employers.

She sat Archie down in a chair and brought over a tin bowl of water with a flannel and dipped it in. After wringing out the excess water, she gently cleansed his elbows and knees and dried them in a towel. 'That should help for time being,' she said. Then she placed a plate of bread and ham in front of him and a cup of tea. 'Are you all right?' She whispered.

He nodded with tears in his eyes but forced a smile at her. How he longed to say he'd been taken against his will by a big bad-tempered old bugger and that he really lived with his Uncle Walter, Cook and Polly in a lovely big house. But who would believe him? It all sounded so far-fetched and if they didn't believe him, what then? He'd get dragged away and beaten by Bill for telling on him. No, thank you very much, he couldn't risk that right now.

Much to his surprise, Bill didn't take him to another house, instead, they ended up in some sort of tavern where the beer was free flowing and the noise loud and raucous. He watched as Bill knocked back several pints but still remained on his feet. He offered Archie a glass of gin, but he refused. 'Have it your own way instead, but don't be such a cissy, lad!'

'I'd rather have a pint of beer!' he found himself saying. He figured it might taste better than the gin and would take him longer to sup.

Bill laughed and hit him hard on the back. 'We'll make a man out of you yet!' he bellowed.

***

Archie awoke to find his face wet and sloppy as he looked up into the looming face of Duke. Where was he? It was all coming back to him now, he'd been up a lot of chimneys yesterday and then Bill had taken him to the pub. He had no memory of how he got home or why he was lying on a big pillow under the table with the dog.

From a distance, he could hear Bill's loud snores and Flora muttering to herself. 'Great big lummox taking the boy out with him on a bender like that!'

He heard Bobby answer her quietly. 'He did the same thing to me, too, on my first day, remember?'

She went over to him and swept him up in her arms. 'Sorry, Bobby. I should never have brought you to live with a beast like him.' She cuddled him close to her bosom.

'It's all right, Ma,' he soothed, and to Archie's horror she began to weep.

So they were mother and son? He'd never reckoned on that. But the question was, was Bobby Bill's son, too? He guessed maybe not. He let out a long groan as he tried to pull himself up.

In a flash, Flora was at his side, kneeling, looking at him under the table. 'I'm so sorry, Archie. Bill shouldn't have taken you to the pub last night.'

'My arms and legs are so sore,' he complained. 'The maid at the big house had to clean my wounds for me.'

'You'll get used to it,' she reassured. 'I'll put brine on you later, then you can stand in front of the fire to harden your skin. I expect you've got a bit of a headache and all?'

He nodded. It felt as though there were a hundred marching soldiers in his brain, 1, 2, 1, 2, about turn!

'You stay there a bit longer, you've got a hangover I expect. I'll fetch you a cup of water.'

What was a hangover? He had no idea, though he did remember Ginny next door saying once that her George was in bed with one.

As if realising his confusion when his mother had gone to get the water, Bobby explained, 'A 'angover is when you've drunk too much alcohol. When you then get an 'eadache and feel sick.'

Archie nodded. 'That's exactly how I feel. So you've had one an' all?'

'Many times,' Bobby said. 'I got used to drinking alcohol in the end though. Bill will get nasty if you refuse, so I've thought of a few tricks to get away with drinking less. Don't much like the taste of it anyhow!'

'Nor me!' Archie agreed. 'So what sort of tricks did you get up to so you didn't have to drink so much?'

'Mainly things like tipping some of my drink into Bill's glass or someone else's...' he said in a hushed tone as he drew up close to Archie for fear of being overheard by Bill. 'Or if I'm not able to do that, sometimes I've tipped some on the floor or let it run down me shirt.'

Archie was beginning to feel for the boy again, even though he'd been well annoyed when he'd dobbed him in to Bill about leaving the place. 'Why did you warn Bill I was about to escape yesterday?'

'I'm sorry about that, mate. I had to do it as Bill reckoned you might make a run for it. Now he trusts me, see, so if in future I lie to him, he'll believe me!'

'That's smart thinking, Nipper!' Archie grinned. Then Flora appeared with a tin mug of cold water. 'Sip it slowly,' she advised as she lifted the tablecloth to pass it to him under the table.

He took the mug from her outstretched hand and thanked her, taking her advice even though he felt like knocking it back all in one go, he was that thirsty.

'Now if you can keep that down for a bit, you can try a slice of bread and butter later…' Truth was he didn't much feel like eating anything at the moment for fear of vomiting up the contents of his stomach. How on earth could he carry on like this? It was hell on earth up those chimneys and then to have to drink as much beer as Bill wanted him to. Yet, he could hardly offend him so he'd have to take the nipper's advice in future. And his throat felt dry and sore and he guessed it was from that soot he'd breathed in yesterday.

Bill let out a loud groan causing Archie to flinch. 'Don't worry none,' Bobby whispered. 'He'll be out cold for ages and you won't have to go up chimneys every day of the week as work can be far and few between.'

Archie scratched his head. 'How'd you mean, like?'

'Well, he's not the most reliable sort, so sometimes he doesn't get asked back. Either that or he argues like hell about payment, tries to pull a flanker by saying the price has gone up! Course the nobs tell their friends then and he finds not many will give him work. Either that or they get wise to stuff going missing from their houses!'

'That's true about the payment as he did that to my uncle. He reckons he kidnapped me as my uncle owes him money.'

Bobby nodded. 'I liked it in that big house but I got sick right after.'

'How old are you?'

'I'll be eight soon.'

Archie swallowed in disbelief. 'Never. I thought you was a lot younger than that.'

Bobby smiled. 'Everyone thinks that. I'm just small for me age, which is why Bill likes shoving me up chimney's so much.'

'So, Flora is your mother, then?'

'Yes, and I don't know why she got involved with a bad 'un like him neither!' He drew a breath. 'The worst of it is when he takes her out drinking with him and they come back home late, he knocks her about as he gets jealous of men looking at her. Even though there's nothing to get jealous about. I can hear him slapping her around behind the curtain.'

For a moment, Archie thought the boy was going to cry, so he tried to say something nice. 'Your ma is very pretty…' Archie said, realising if he was grown up and had a nice lady like her in his life, he'd be certain to treat her with the utmost respect.

'Yes, she is, but I've seen fellas looking at her and well, Bill, he ain't blind, he notices an' all. That's part of the problem really, why he knocks her around. He's mad with jealousy. I saw him knock a bloke out once just because he smiled at me ma in the street.'

Archie shook his head. 'Well, I'm here now so if he starts his capers, I'll step in.'

'But yer only a boy like me,' Bobby said.

'Yes, but if I heard him striking your ma after she's been so kind to me, I'd have to do something.'

'Ma begged him not to kidnap you, Archie, but he warned her if she didn't help and keep her gob shut he'd have me by the throat and squeeze so hard I'd pass out!' Bobby shut his eyes firmly as if the thought of what Bill could do to him was all too much to bear. As if Duke realised what was happening, he came over to the lads and started licking Bobby's face.

'Don't you worry none,' Archie reassured, 'I won't let him hurt you either, Bobby. What kind of dog is Duke? I've never seen one like him before. He's really big!'

'Ma says he's an Irish Wolfhound. Bill always tells people he's a nasty dog and makes him growl, but he's soft as butter.' He chuckled, then put both hands to his mouth in case he woke Bill. It was obvious the longer Bill slept the better it would be for everyone.

***

By evening time there was still no sign of Archie, so Cook was forced to tell the master. She tapped softly on the drawing-room door, half hoping that Archie might turn up at the final hour. Polly exchanged worried glances with her.

'Enter!' Walter shouted from his desk, where he was seated. He looked up from some sort of ledger he was reading as she and Polly stepped into the room. 'Everything all right with tonight's meal, Mrs Stockley?'

Cook wrung her hands together, her palms were perspiring profusely and her mouth was dry. 'Yes, sir. It's not the meal we've come to see you about.'

'Oh?' He blinked several times.

'It's about young Archie, sir…'

'Yes? Isn't he able to dine with me tonight?'

'Well, no, sir. Not really.'

The master was beginning to look amused. 'You mean he has other things to do? More important than eating a meal with his uncle?'

'No, sir, it's not that. It's just when Polly went to wake him this morning, she couldn't find him. He wasn't in his bedroom or anywhere else in the house for that matter. We waited until now in case he's been playing in the woods or something and forgotten the time or maybe he got himself lost in the grounds.'

Walter's eyes enlarged and his lips were set in a fine line. Oh dear! She'd seen that look before when he got angry. 'And pray tell me why you both waited until now to inform me?' He steepled his fingers.

'Well, you have been in London on business, sir, it would have been hard to contact you anyhow.' She huffed out a breath realising she was right.

He appeared to think about it for a moment and he rubbed his chin. 'But a boy doesn't just disappear in the middle of the night,' he said, frowning.

'We think someone must have taken him from his bed, sir. He'd never have run away in his nightshirt, dressing gown and slippers when there were perfectly good clothes and boots he could have put on instead!'

'But he didn't much like his new clobber,' Polly butted in. 'He thought the frilly shirt made him look like such a cissy!' Cook glared at her as if she had spoken out of turn.

'I see,' Walter said. 'I think you're probably right, Mrs Stockley. We need to get the police involved in this. Who would want to take him away though?'

'Maybe someone from the East End like that Ginny woman he was always talking about? Maybe she missed him something rotten.'

'Possibly,' said Walter, 'though I did meet her to make the funeral arrangements and she didn't seem to be that sort of person. She was most helpful actually. And I know she couldn't have possibly afforded to feed another mouth. So really, I don't think he's with her somehow.'

'Perhaps someone knowing the boy is here wanted him and they'll demand money for his return!' Polly blurted out.

Walter narrowed his eyes. 'How do you know so much about that sort of thing?'

Polly's face flushed. 'Sorry, sir. I was letting me imagination run away with me. I read a newspaper story once about it.'

'Well, what happened in the story?' Cook nudged her.

'A young boy was kidnapped, he lived with a wealthy family and threats were made that if the master of the house didn't pay up their son would be killed. And I'm sorry to say…'

'Yes?' Walter said, waiting in expectation.

'It was not a happy ending. The family couldn't raise the money in time and the boy was found floating down the river…'

'Aw, that poor young lad!' Cook shouted. 'Whoever did that ought to be horsewhipped!'

Walter put his head in his hands and for a moment Cook feared he'd break down crying, but then he looked at them both and said, 'I think I need to involve the police in this right away. The sooner I see them the better.'

**

Bill slept most of the day and the expression on Flora's face was a picture. It seemed to Archie that she looked fraught with indecision and anxiety about something as she constantly chewed on her bottom lip and frowned.

'What's wrong?' he asked. He had now crawled out from beneath the table and was seated with Bobby at the table. His limbs still ached something rotten and his elbows and knees were extremely sore, but his stomach now felt more normal, which he was most grateful for. He dreaded to think what would have happened if he'd drunk the gin as well.

'I'm debating whether the three of us should make a run for it,' she whispered.

'But what about Duke?' Bobby questioned.

'I've thought about that, but don't know of any lodging houses what would take a dog, never mind a big 'un like him.' She looked at her son's crestfallen face and Archie noticed tears in her eyes.

'Your ma's right. If we leave here we'll get spotted if we have a big dog with us.'

Bobby nodded, seeming to understand, then he brightened as he said, 'What about that landlady downstairs in the pub? We could ask her to take care of him until it's safe to come back here for him.'

Flora shook her head. 'If we leave, we tell no one.'

Suddenly, there was a loud grunt as Bill stirred and Archie could see the man pulling himself bolt upright through a chink in the curtain.

'What time is it, woman?'

'Half past three, Bill,' she replied, her voice sounding thin and shaky.

'That's all? I've have another forty winks then,' he said, as he settled himself back down to sleep. Archie guessed it would no longer be safe to discuss any escape plans for fear he wasn't really asleep, so he and Bobby spent their time playing with the marbles the lad had produced from his pocket.

He hoped there'd eventually be some sort of a chance to escape this place and get well away from Bill's clutches. Flora and Bobby especially deserved a place of safety. Even Duke, who whimpered every so often as if he knew there was something amiss, deserved his freedom too.

Chapter Seven

Walter Brooking and his staff were interviewed by a surly detective who introduced himself as Inspector Arthur Reid. Reid was accompanied by a young uniformed policeman. The pair were quite a contrast, like chalk and cheese. No one in the house had a clue what had happened to Archie and Cook blamed herself for the lad's disappearance. Later, she and Polly took a well-earned break in the kitchen in front of a roaring fire. It had been quite a cold day so far. She hoped wherever the boy was that he had food and shelter, she couldn't bear anything to happen to him.

'I should have kept more of an eye on the lad...' Cook said, then she took a sip of her tea. She was sitting in the armchair nearest the fireplace whilst Polly rocked slowly back and forth in the rocking chair for a change.

'Now don't go blaming yourself, Mrs Stockley!' Polly said. She was in the middle of embroidering a handkerchief. 'I'm stitching this 'specially for Archie for his safe return! I've stitched an A into each corner.'

Cook smiled. 'You create such beautiful needlework, Poll, you're a dab hand with a needle and thread. I suppose we both tried to look out for him, even Mr Featherstone, but to no avail. How did we know he was going to go missing in the middle of the night? I've a good mind to—'

Polly stopped rocking for a moment. 'To what?'

Cook shook her head. 'It's silly I suppose, but if I can find that Ginny woman who was his neighbour, I could ask if she might have seen him. Maybe the lad has returned home without saying, like. Maybe the master is wrong about that. Archie was very fond of the woman.'

'I think that's unlikely, Mrs Stockley! Where would he go for a start? And how would he know how to get there? He had no money. Can't see it meself.'

Cook clucked her teeth. 'Aye, maybe you're right, Poll. Don't go listening to the ramblings of an old woman.'

'Anyhow, those policemen said there would be a thorough search of the grounds first thing in the morning at first light, to see if there are any clues. I'm sure they'll check things out with that Ginny woman and all, the master did mention her and the street Archie'd lived in to the police.'

Cook closed her eyes as if she wanted to block out the bad stuff that had been going on. At the moment all she could see was Archie's face before her and she sensed that wherever he was, he was in big trouble.

***

'Get up that bleedin' chimney, you flamin' young upstart!' Bill growled.

Archie didn't like it at all. Bill's previous good mood from the day before had worn off and now he'd decided he could work faster with two chimney sweeps, which might have been the case except for the fact that poor Bobby still wasn't up to it. Archie could see the fear in the boy's eyes.

'It's all right, Mr Brackley, I can clear all the chimneys today, I'm fit and strong, the nipper can wait down below with the dust sheets. It will make the maids and the master more sympathetic if they keep him in view and they might give us more to eat.'

'Maybe you're right,' Bill said rubbing his chin. 'But when you're up to it, I want you back up there, no complaint, you whippersnapper!' He roughly pushed Bobby to one side with such force the boy almost toppled over.

Archie winked at the boy and Bobby sported a shaky smile back at him.

'No slacking now!' Bill ordered. 'While yer waiting, Bobby, look what we can pilfer from the room. Remember what I said now, don't whip nothing that'll be noticed immediately as gorn missing. Got to keep our wits about us.' He tapped the side of his nose.

Now that Archie knew what do it seemed a bit better today, scrambling up a chimney, especially as Flora had brined him the night before. She'd brushed his elbows and knees in a brine solution and stood him in front of the fire telling him it would help to harden his skin.

'Make sure you wear your cap and a hanky or scarf around your nose and mouth as they're your only protection if any soot should fall on top of you.' What she hadn't told him was that a big fall of soot could suffocate him or that sometimes young boys became trapped in chimneys. Bobby had warned him of that as he in turn had been told by an older lad who once worked for Bill. The boy was too big to work for him any more so Bill had sold him on to an undertaker as an apprentice. Living in the city wasn't easy for young lads, Archie thought.

Archie heaved himself up inside the chimney breast and he used the metal scraper and a brush like Bill had told him to, but after a while, he could get no further up the chimney as it was so narrow. Much narrower than any chimney he'd climbed the day before. He got himself back down to tell Bill.

'You can try going up in yer birthday suit instead!' he cackled.

Birthday suit? What did the man mean?

'Naked,' Bobby explained.

'Or I can send young Bobby up instead as he's that much smaller!'

Bill's wicked taunt really got to Archie as the lad just wasn't well enough and the man knew it. There was no question about it, he was going to have to climb up naked. He didn't want to subject poor Bobby to that, the lad was too frail.

He stripped off his clothing and was about to go up, just as a maid entered the room. 'The mistress is asking if…' she almost fainted from shock when she saw Archie stood there in the nude.

Archie blushed and turned his head away from the woman.

'Sorry missus,' Bill explained, 'needs must. This chimney has quite a narrow breast, it's the only way I can get it swept for you and the other little lad has been so poorly.'

'Aw, has he now?' said the middle-aged maid, her eyes full of compassion.

Bill sure knew how to pull on the heartstrings. 'His ma's gorn to heaven to be with the angels…only last month.'

'Oh you poor boy,' said the maid. She had a different accent to what Archie was used to, Irish he thought, there'd been a man living in his street who worked at the docks who had a similar accent, all soft and sing-song like.

'I was going to ask you,' the maid explained, 'if you wanted anything to eat later? You must be hungry for sure?'

'That would be nice of you, ma'am,' Bill said, the whites of his eyes showing. 'None of us has eaten much for days as the work's been drying up so if you could ask your mistress if she could inform all her friends about our services?'

The maid nodded. 'When you've finished here, come to the kitchen and Cook will have something ready for you.'

Archie was astonished how Bill could accept the mistress's benevolence whilst at the same time pilfer her belongings! What a rat. He watched as the maid left the room and he was sure she sniffed back a tear. That was an out and out lie about none of them eating for days, too. All right, it wasn't the best of grub but they did have food in their bellies.

'Don't just stand there gawping, Archie, get back up that chimney! The sooner you finish what you came to do the sooner we can all eat!' he bellowed.

Climbing up the chimney in the buff wasn't easy and his skin was more prone to cuts and scrapes. Being unclothed did give him a bit of leeway but it was so claustrophobic in such a confining space. Sometimes it felt like he could hardly breathe at all as his ribcage was so close to the brickwork, and he realised if he panicked he'd make things a whole lot worse for himself, so he tried to keep his mind on other things. What about when he got bigger though? He'd already outgrown his clothing in the past few weeks. The thought of him helping Bobby, and Flora too in a way, for she would not want to see her sick young boy climbing any more chimneys, spurred him on. And when he thought he wanted to get out, he imagined the awaiting grub in the kitchen as his reward. He wondered if that cook was as good as his cook back at the big house.

The chimney was so tricky with lots of twists and turns and not being able to see much at all made it even more difficult. He feared he'd get lost but he managed to feel his way out, knowing where certain shaped bricks were. Finally, he got himself to the bottom of the chimney and clambered out of the grate. Wheezing a great deal, he found he could hardly see as his eyelashes were covered in soot and he'd suffered even more scrapes than the day before. There was no sign of Bill or Bobby and he was just about to get himself dressed when the maid returned.

'Goodness me!' she said, 'on God's green earth I've never seen such a sight, you're like a minstrel boy, you are! Let me fetch ye a bowl of warm water and some soap. Best clean you up in the scullery though or the mistress won't be too pleased with great mucky splodges over her best carpet and furniture, it might get through the dust sheets. T'aint right you making the place look dirty, young man!' She'd said the words with a hint of humour so Archie knew she wasn't really annoyed. How could she be? He'd just risked life and limb to sweep that blessed chimney.

Finally, he could see. The maid who'd told him her name was Edna had gently wiped the soot from his eyes and was now flannelling his face, arms and body as he stood near the scullery back door. She ended up changing the water a couple of times in the process. 'It's a pity now I've cleaned you up that you have to wear those dirty clothes again,' she grumbled. Then her face broke out into a grin. 'I have an idea!' She said, holding up her index finger, her green eyes shining like two emeralds. 'There was a young lad who used to work here, got into trouble for stealing from the master, he left a set of clothing behind, he was just a bit bigger than you. I'll go and fetch them!'

'You'd better check with Mr Brackley before you give them to me,' Archie advised.

Edna nodded and returned within minutes with a pair of over-the-knee breeches that didn't even have a tear in them. A striped shirt, waistcoat and a little jacket. 'You'll look right smart in these,' she said. 'I've also managed to find something for the younger lad. Me son lives here and he's outgrown his clothes, so Bobby can have those.'

When he was nice and clean and dressed, Edna sat him at the table and placed a plate of ham and pickles and a hunk of bread in front of him. Should he risk telling her he shouldn't really be here at all, he wondered? He could hear Bill's voice out in the corridor and signs he and Bobby had already been fed as there were two plates and two tin mugs on the table.

He was just about to say something when Edna asked, 'Would you like a cup of buttermilk, lad?'

'Yes, please.' Why was she so kind to him? Maybe it was a blessing because if he told her about what had happened to him, she might tell her master and mistress who would surely fetch the police.

'I can't keep calling you "lad". What's your name?' She furrowed her brow.

He was just about to answer 'Archie' when Bill swept into the room, 'His name is Ronald, but we call him Ronnie!' He slapped Archie hard on the back. It was obvious that he didn't want to give any information away. 'Hurry up and eat that food now, Ronnie!' Bill urged. 'We have another house to get to!'

Archie realised that was an out and out lie. There were no more chimneys to be swept today, thankfully. He was trying to get him off the premises before questions were asked.

'I'll just go and get your payment,' Edna said. When she'd left the room Bill grabbed Archie by the scruff of the neck. 'Don't go getting any ideas about spillin' yer guts to the likes of her, mind!'

Bill's rotting teeth made his breath smell something bad, even worse than usual today, and Archie recoiled. 'N...no, sir...'

Then he suddenly released him as he heard approaching voices, he softened his voice. 'Yer done well today, lad,' he said, patting Archie's head as if he was a good dog as Edna returned with an envelope.

'The mistress says she will most definitely recommend your services to her friends, Mr Brackley,' Edna said.

'Thank you, ma'am.' Bill tipped his battered top hat. Then clearing his throat glared at Archie as if to say, 'Come on, let's get out of here!'

He had gulped down some of the food but pocketed the remainder for fear Bill might stop him from eating it. He drank the buttermilk down in one go and, thanking the maid, wiped his mouth with the back of his hand. Pity he didn't have a clean handkerchief, he thought.

***

'I've finished the hankie for Archie!' Polly said, holding it up for Cook to inspect her handiwork.

'My, you've a real touch with embroidery, Poll,' Cook said. 'That's lovely. Those policemen have arrived and they're searching the grounds as we speak.' She looked out the window to see there were five of them, all in uniform, except for one who wore a long dark frock coat and smoked a pipe, she recognised him as Detective Inspector Reid from the day before.

'I can't see what they could possibly find that would help locate him though,' Polly frowned.

'Well they have to try, haven't they?' Cook sniffed. 'The master seems right down about it all. He told me he'd promised his sister he'd take care of the boy. It's not his fault if the lad has decided to run off.'

'We don't know that, do we?' said Polly.

Cook clucked her teeth.

It was another couple of hours before the detective asked to see Mr Brooking. The master ushered the officer into his study whilst Polly listened by the door.

'What's he saying?' Cook urged.

'I can't hear much but something has been found somewhere,' Polly hissed.

Cook wondered what it could possibly be. She waited with bated breath as Polly listened for a while longer, but spotting Mrs Linley in the distance down the corridor, Cook grabbed hold of Polly's arm. 'We better go, that old crone Linley is heading this way.'

Polly nodded and walked off with Cook in the direction of the kitchen. They'd find out what it was in due course.

***

Archie and Bobby were seated at the pub whilst Bill was by the long bar chatting with some of his mates. Archie's dirty clothing was rolled up in a bundle tied with string at his side. Bobby had his new clothes tied up too, but wasn't wearing his new stuff as he hadn't had a good scrub like Archie. Archie felt the most normal he had in days; it was nice to feel clean for once.

It was a long time until Bill returned from the bar with a tankard of ale each for them. The longer he stopped away the better as the boys really didn't want to drink the stuff, but this time Archie had to admit he felt thirsty after being up that chimney and could well see how a young sweep got into drinking alcohol, especially as it helped to soothe a sore throat.

He took a long swig in front of Bill as he knew it would please him, and so did Bobby, but when the man turned back to the bar, they thought of ways to get rid of the offending stuff. Archie didn't want to risk another hangover he had to keep his wits about him. Duke was tied up under the table and seemed quite docile as if he realised his master was in a good mood.

Bill looked at them both and said, 'Don't you dare try getting away neither, I've trained that dog to bark at you!'

Archie didn't know if this were true or not but decided he didn't want to risk it even if the dog didn't seem that fierce. Bill had left an old sack beside them they were to guard with their lives, it contained some valuables from the house they'd just swept. No wonder Bill never got asked back, he reckoned. If the house owners didn't find out stuff was missing whilst they were there, they would surely do so in due course.

'How did your ma get with Bill in the first place?' Archie asked. He was curious to know how a lovely lady like Flora could end up with a brute like Bill.

Bobby frowned. 'She was working as a barmaid in the pub we're staying at. Bill promised her the world but in the end she got nuffink 'cept a load of grief...'

Archie nodded. 'What happened to your father, if you don't mind me asking?'

'He was a sailor but got lost at sea. There's not many men want to take on a young woman and a little boy, so me ma thought she was in God's pocket when she met Bill. But I reckon it were all planned. He took her on as he knew given time I could work for him.'

'What makes you think that?' Archie took another sup of beer forgetting he needed to keep off the stuff.

'Bill's had more than one woman in his life and the last apprentice who got too big to go up chimneys any more was the lad of one of Bill's women.'

Archie nodded. Thank goodness his mother hadn't met someone like him! It seemed to him that Bill was deliberately setting his cap at young women who had young sons who could make brass for him.

It was getting dark by the time the trio and Duke returned home. Flora was waiting for them sitting by the table, her eyes looking red raw like she'd been crying, but Archie noticed some sliced onions on a plate. 'I've made you all a nice pie!' she declared, wiping her eyes with the back of her hand.

'Where'd you get the money from to make it, woman?' Bill growled.

Flora hesitated. 'Connie had some onions to spare and a bit o' meat. It's a bit gristly, but it will fill our bellies for a bit.'

'Who's Connie?' Archie whispered to Bobby.

'The landlady downstairs.'

Bill narrowed his eyes. 'Did yer pay her anything?'

'N..No, Bill. I helped her in the bar for a bit and she gave me it as payment.'

Bill's eyes flashed dangerously. 'What have I told you about working in the bar? You're with me now so I don't want you flashing your breasts in front of the punters.'

'I didn't, Bill, I kept meself covered up, honestly. I had my shawl wrapped around me shoulders. And now we've got a nice pie and some spuds out of me work this afternoon.'

'I suppose it'll do,' he said, drawing back a chair to sit down at the table.

Bobby let out a long breath as if pleased Bill wasn't about to kick off.

'Next time,' said Bill, 'you check with me first whether or not you can work in the bar.'

'All right, Bill,' Flora said meekly. Then turning to the boys, 'Sit yourselves down and I'll fetch the plates.'

Archie could hardly believe his good fortune to get well fed twice in one day. But he knew to be wary of Bill and to keep him on side; he wasn't daft.

The pie wasn't as good as Cook's back at the big house, but it was tasty all the same, even if the meat was a bit chewy. Even Duke managed to have a few bits of burnt crust and gristle which he ate with relish. They all had full bellies going to bed and feeling the best since he got there, he and Bobby curled up with Duke in the corner.

He didn't know how long he'd been asleep for when Archie heard whimpering sounds.

'Come on now, woman, give me what's me right!' It was Bill's voice.

'Please Bill, I'm so tired,' Flora complained.

'Well yer know what you'll get if you refuse, me love,' he heard Bill say.

There was no more whimpering after that and Archie could hear the sounds of the bed springs squeaking and after a couple of minutes, even though he had his fingers plugged into his ears, he heard Bill let out a long, loud groan. What had happened there he had no idea but it wasn't long before Bill was snoring loudly. He pretended to be asleep himself as Flora dragged herself out of bed and started boiling up a kettle on the fire and some pans on the stove.

She seemed to be pouring the hot water into the small tin bath, then he heard the sounds of splashing as if she was washing herself all over. Whatever had gone on, he knew that woman wasn't happy at all.

***

The master summoned all his staff together, including Archie's tutors. 'The police have searched the grounds,' he said solemnly, 'and have found something.'

There was a long pause as the detective glared at them all as if they were culprits which made Cook's tummy flip over even though she knew she'd done no wrong whatsoever.

'Can you tell us what exactly you found then?' Cook asked, causing Mrs Linley to glare at her as if she had been extremely impudent for interrupting the detective. Taking no notice of the woman, she said, 'We need to know.'

Mr Brooking turned to the detective, 'Is that all right, Mr Reid?'

The detective nodded.

'A garment was found smeared in blood, near the trees…' Mr Brooking said.

'Oh, me giddy aunt,' said Polly.

Cook said nothing, just stood there, she had to know more. 'What sort of garment?'

'Do you recognise this?' the detective held up a piece of blue candy-striped flannelette.

Cook narrowed her gaze.

'That looks like part of Archie's nightshirt!' Polly piped up.

'Yes, it most certainly is,' Cook agreed.

Mr Brooking glanced at the detective. 'I fear the worst,' he said.

'Have you had any unusual callers to the house lately?' The detective asked, taking a puff on his pipe, filling the air with acrid smoke.

'Not really,' said the master. 'My usual business associates and one or two tradesmen…'

Cook didn't want to say it but the look on Polly's face was such a picture to behold as Mr Brooking spoke about the girl's uncle. 'There was a chimney sweep who came here, Inspector. He went away with a flea in his ear as he reckoned I owed him more money. I didn't think too much about it at the time.'

'I'm sorry, Poll, I have to say this,' Cook whispered. Then she turned to the master and the Inspector. 'The boy, Archie, was scared stiff of the sweep. His name is Mr Brackley. He had a young 'un with him who was spluttering and wheezing all the time.'

Polly's face went red. 'He's my uncle, Inspector.'

'Where does he live?' The Inspector looked at the maid with grave concern in his eyes.

'I don't rightly know as he moves around a lot, sir. The last time he had somewhere to stay was a doss house down by the docks but I'm sure he told me he'd left there and gone to lodgings at some pub, but I can't remember the name of it.'

'That narrows it down a bit,' said Mrs Linley in a sarcastic fashion as she stood with one hand crossed over the other.

Stuck up, old bag! Cook thought to herself. *I have to say something.* 'That was very unhelpful of you, Mrs Linley. Can you imagine what it must be like for young Polly, here?'

Mrs Linley's gaze was unwavering. 'She shouldn't have brought that man to this house. I never liked him in the first place!' Her chin jutted out in defiance.

'But aren't *you* the person who employed the man, Mrs Linley?' Cook narrowed her eyes then turned away from the woman and back to the detective, for fear she'd say or do something she'd regret. 'Come to think of it, I remember the man talking to Archie and the boy looked petrified.'

The Inspector puffed thoughtfully on his pipe, then removing it from his mouth said, 'Do you know what he actually said to the boy?'

'Sorry, no idea, sir. But whatever it was it seemed to scare the living daylights out of him!'

Polly's shoulders shuddered as if she was about to cry, so Cook took her hand as a sign of reassurance. At least now they'd patched up their differences and were singing from the same hymn sheet.

The police had a new lead but where would it take them? It was like looking for a needle up a chimney stack when chimneys and sweeps in the city were ten a penny.

Chapter Eight

The following day it really did appear as if Flora had been crying this time and Archie just knew it had something to do with the night before. He could tell the poor young woman didn't have much of a life, but what could he do about it? He was only a boy. Still, he didn't like to see her upset. Bobby didn't seem too bothered about it, it was as if he was used to such goings-on in his young life.

Bill, on the other hand, woke up in a good mood asking for his breakfast. He'd brought a package of sausages back with him that he'd bought off some man in the pub the day before, so Flora fried those and they had some with a slice of bread and dripping. She'd even fried some leftover onions for them as well, but Archie declined those as he had drunk more than he intended at the pub the previous day and felt very bloated indeed.

If it wasn't for the fact that Flora seemed so downcast and upset he'd have been in a good mood himself that morning. He'd done well climbing up that chimney yesterday and was quite proud of himself, though it wasn't something he'd want to do for long. Couldn't do in any case as he knew he was growing so fast that another few months and maybe he'd not fit into any more small chimneys.

Bill ate his breakfast heartily, devouring more sausages than anyone else. He belched loudly at the end of his feast, then he slapped Flora hard on the backside and demanded, 'Tea, woman!'

She nodded meekly and went off to pour them all some tea. There were only two mugs available, one each for Flora and Bill, so Archie and Bobby shared a saucer of tea between them.

'You want to keep those new clothes for best, Archie,' Flora said, as she joined them at the table. 'They'll be nice for going to church.'

Bill glanced at him, his eyes lighting up. 'I could maybe sell those to the dolly shop or at the market!'

Flora's eyes clouded over. 'No, Bill. Let the lad keep them, he might need them if you sell him on. He needs to look respectable.' Archie could tell that Flora was just softening Bill up and she wouldn't want him sold on, she cared about his safety but she'd say anything to butter Bill up.

'Aye, maybe you're right and all!' He said, then he took a loud slurp of his tea and gasped. Archie hated the way the man drank his tea like a pig with its snout in a trough, he had no manners at all. 'Now being the benevolent chap what I am, I'm giving you the day off today, Archie, but I'm taking young Bobby out with me instead.'

'Oh, no, please don't, Bill!' Flora's eyes were wide with horror.

He smiled. 'No, it's nothing like that so don't worry at all. I won't be sending him up no chimneys today. I've just realised that when people see the lad they feel sorry for him especially as he's so wiry looking and full of melancholy. I can get more money by taking him door-to-door I reckon and telling them how his ma has gorn to live with the angels.' He held the palms of his hands together as if in prayer and looked heavenward.

The bleeding heathen that he was! What a blooming liar!

Flora huffed out a breath of relief. 'Please look after him then, Bill.'

He nodded. Then he turned to Archie. 'Now as I'm giving you a day off, me lad, I want you to keep an eye on this woman when I'm gone. She's not to fornicate in the bar downstairs. Do you understand?'

He had no idea what the word "fornicate" meant, but he nodded anyhow.

Bill rose from the table and then ruffled Bobby's hair. 'Go and get ready, wear them new clothes the maid gave you but don't go washing yerself, we still want you to look like a poor orphan boy.'

'Yes, sir.' Bobby smiled, obviously pleased he wouldn't be forced up any chimneys today.

When they'd both departed, taking Duke with them, Flora turned to Archie. 'I would tell you to run for your life, Archie, but if I do that, my boy is with Bill and he could hurt him if he returns knowing I've purposely allowed you to leave here.'

Archie looked at her in earnest. 'Please don't worry, Flora. I understand that. I am going to stay, but one day we'll take our chance and all get out of here.' He longed to ask her about what had happened last night but he felt he couldn't, it would be a bit forward of him.

So instead, he helped Flora take the dishes over to the sink where she boiled the kettle and washed them. He didn't even have Duke to keep him company, so he sat in the corner playing marbles until Flora had finished the dishes, then she said to him, 'How would you like me to tell you a story?'

No one had told him a story before except for his mother, so he brightened up and nodded. Flora settled herself in the armchair as she told him such fantastical tales about witches and fairies and elves and goblins. He found himself hanging on to her every word and when she'd finished, he said. 'I enjoyed that, but which book did you get that story from?'

Flora beamed at him. 'I didn't, Archie. I wrote it myself. See here…' She stood and walked over to a coal sack Bobby had been lying on, on the floor, where she brought out a book that looked like an old ledger of sorts. 'Connie from the pub gave it to me and I've been writing stories down in it.'

Archie gasped when he saw her beautiful penmanship. 'I bet you're surprised I'm educated, aren't you?'

'Oh, no,' said Archie, when in reality he was very surprised indeed.

'I went to school and all, but I had to leave when my father died. We didn't have any more money for my education, times were hard, and a few years later I got pregnant with Bobby.'

'What would you have liked to have done then, Flora?'

'I think I'd liked to have been an author of children's books, but that's never likely to happen. I also enjoyed working as a barmaid as I met lots of people. But Bill didn't like that as he got jealous, still does. It's annoying as I could earn meself a bit of money if I worked downstairs but he won't hear of it! So, my only pleasure is writing stories when he's out and I keep them well hidden away from his eyes.'

Archie could feel her frustration. Here was a woman who obviously wanted to better herself in life but Bill was having none of it. If he found that book he guessed the man would be so jealous that he'd tear it apart, no wonder Flora kept it hidden. And the reason she wanted to better herself was probably to give her son a better life that didn't involve scrambling up chimneys. Sometimes life was so unfair.

***

The police had been to visit Ginny, who apparently had been most concerned for Archie's welfare, but no, she herself hadn't set eyes on him. But she'd said if he showed up she'd contact them.

So that left Cook and Polly none the wiser.

'If me uncle has got him I'm sure he won't harm him none,' said Polly, as she helped Cook to peel the spuds for the evening meal.

Cook leaned over to take the roast out of the oven. She placed the sizzling baking tray on the wooden counter, stuck a long fork into it, inspected it thoroughly, sniffed its aroma and returned it to its hot furnace. 'Needs about another twenty minutes,' she said confidently. 'Let's hope you're right, Polly. Your heart's in the right place but you can be so naïve at times!'

'What do yer mean?' Polly was so taken aback by Cook's remark that she dropped her knife into the bowl of water.

'Well it's obvious that man makes a living off small children and what he does isn't right in my book. There's a law that's been passed by Parliament so he shouldn't be doing it in the first place!'

Polly shrugged her shoulders. 'Then if that's the bleeding case shouldn't some of those rich folks be fined or be behind bars for encouraging it? After all, if it wasn't for their sort young boys wouldn't be forced up those big chimneys in the first place!'

Cook realised that maybe Polly had a point there but she wasn't bound to agree with her. Instead she changed the subject. 'At least the master's dining at home this evening with a guest.'

'He's got that Mrs Pearson, the merry widow woman, around again!'

Cook chuckled. 'Well, he's entitled to a bit of life, even if the woman sees him as her next husband and he's too daft to notice!' In truth though, she was pleased the master had some company to stop him fretting even if she thought the woman wanted to dig her claws into him.

***

Bill and Bobby had been gone for hours and Flora was beginning to get anxious. She'd made a stew with some of the leftover meat, a bit of bone, and some onion and carrots topped off with several dumplings, which was ready long since. 'I hope Bill hasn't taken Bobby to the pub again,' she said, then chewed on her bottom lip.

'Does he do it that often?' Archie wanted to know.

'I'm afraid so. It's more often than not.'

'You should have left him a long time ago, Flora.'

Flora shook her head. 'I did a time or two, but he'd find me and drag me back home by me hair, then I'd get a hammering for going and a hammering for coming back, I just couldn't win. Then his mind would work overtime, accusing me of all sorts. I'm sorry, I shouldn't be burdening you with all of this, lad. You're too young.'

'I think I get it,' he said. He touched her arm. 'You're very nice, Flora. I wish you could meet someone lovely instead.'

'Maybe someday,' she said. Then she went to fill the kettle. 'It's no use us fretting, I'll make us a cup of tea.'

'Will you read me another story, please?'

She nodded. 'Aye, go on then.' Flora was pleased to have an appreciative audience for her work and Archie was only too pleased to be that person. 'I'll tear a couple of pages out of the book so you can draw something to keep yourself amused after I've read to you,' she said softly

Flora was halfway through a third story when Bill turned up hiccupping as he pushed Bobby in through the door ahead of him, Archie quickly cleared things away. 'This young lad has done wonders for us today. I've made some good money out of him. I'm thinking of selling him on to Frobisher, the undertaker, where the other lad got sold to. He looks so angelic.' He hiccupped again.

Bobby was beaming, pleased that he was now in Bill's good books but Archie wondered whether Flora would be happier for her son to be working for an undertaker rather than staying at home with them with the possibility of still cleaning chimneys. If she was worried, she deliberately wasn't showing Bill. He had noticed that her expression often changed when she was out of Bill's eyeline.

'I've made some stew for our tea,' Flora said brightly.

'Stuff that!' said Bill. 'I'm taking you out to the chop house, the lads can have the stew. Put on your best dress, Flora!'

Flora smiled, looking happy for once. 'At least there'll be more grub for you and Bobby,' she said, smiling at the boys. 'Now's your chance to get away, Archie,' she advised when Bill had left the room to go downstairs to use the privy.

Something though told him to stay and he was glad that he did.

***

There was a loud bang as the door was thrown open. It was too dark to see immediately, but Archie could tell by the heavy breathing and alcoholic fumes, it was Bill home from the pub. But where was Flora?

He heard him crashing down on his bed and soon he was snoring away. Archie checked on Bobby, who was fast asleep in the corner. Duke whimpered as if he knew something was up.

'Sssh,' said Archie, who by now was on his feet and headed towards the door which he discovered to his amazement, was still open. He could go now if he wanted to, Bill was out of it. But he could never leave Bobby knowing that his mother hadn't come home yet.

Slowly, he crept down the stairs. The pub was in darkness below as he felt his way around, then he heard heavy breaths coming from the corner of the tap room.

'Come on Flora, I'm paying Bill for the privilege, love, let me have a fumble in yer drawers…'

'No, leave me alone, you brute!' he heard her shout at the man and a sound as if she was slapping away at him.

Instinctively, Archie reached out on to the bar and found a large empty bottle of some kind and took it in his hand as slowly he walked to where the noise was coming from.

'Come on, darlin' give a man a bit of pleasure!' he heard the man's excited voice.

Then he sensed things were getting out of hand as he heard Flora squeal as if she was being held down. 'If you won't give it to me then I'll take it, me lovely!'

'No, please, no!' he heard Flora shouting in a state of panic.

As Archie approached and his eyes became more accustomed to the light he could see a large form moving up and down on top of Flora, he lifted the bottle and smashed it hard across the man's head.

'What the hell?' he heard the man cry out.

Then Archie lifted a hard wooden stool and bashed it down on the man again. The man rolled off Flora and toppled with a thud to the floor.

'Archie!' Flora sobbed.

'Come on, we need to get out of here,' he said. 'I might have killed him!'

'No, I doubt it, he's just stunned but you're right. You get Duke and I'll get Bobby. Is Bill asleep yet?'

'Yes, he's well out of it.'

Quietly they tiptoed upstairs and Flora gently roused a sleepy Bobby whilst Archie put on his shoes and took Duke by the lead. He put his jacket on top of his rough work clothes and carried the bundle of new clothing the maid had given him. Then remembering Flora's book of stories, he found it still in the coal sack and tucked it under his arm. Meanwhile, Flora rifled through Bill's jacket which was slung over the table to see if she could find any money. Within minutes they were all safely out of the pub and standing on the pavement outside. The street was mainly in darkness except for a gas lamp at the end of the road. In the distance, he could hear someone singing off key as if they'd had a night at some pub or another.

'Come on, let's get well away from here!' Archie said. He feared both Bill and the bloke he'd hit over the head coming after them. Breathlessly, they scurried across the street and down an alleyway with Duke at their heels. When they felt they'd got far enough away, Flora said, 'I don't know where we can go now.' She paused to take a breath.

'Well, I haven't even any idea where we are!' Archie said.

'The only place I can think of at this hour is to bed down at Itchy Park,' Flora said thoughtfully. 'We'll have to be careful though as there are some rough sorts that doss down there. But if we can all get a bit of kip, when it's first light we can look for a room somewhere.'

'Maybe we could ask that maid who gave me and Bobby those clothes if she can help us, if I can find the house,' Archie said.

Bobby tugged on his jacket sleeve. 'I remember where it is as we've swept a few chimneys in that street.'

'All right then,' Flora announced. 'we'll sleep in Itchy Park tonight, Duke will guard us all, then come first light we'll find that house and speak to the maid.'

***

The park was surrounded by spiked iron railings and was not the sort of park Archie had been expecting. This was more like a churchyard, instead of the pretty park with fragrant fresh flowers like he'd imagined. The only fragrance here was of unwashed bodies and the strong whiff of alcohol that made him want to gag.

As they entered, he saw beneath the moon's silvery light a mass of bodies strewn here and there, and for a moment, he feared they were dead, after all, it was some sort of churchyard. But then he heard some coughs and splutters and the sound of a young baby's wails.

He felt the crunch of gravel beneath his boots and noticed what he thought was a bundle of rags move on a wooden bench. He flinched. And in the background he noticed the shadow of the church with its spire fall across them.

This seemed to him like hell on earth, but maybe it wasn't at all. Maybe hell on earth would be a young child trapped in a hot, sooty, confined space like a chimney breast, knowing full well the master chimney sweep was waiting down below expecting him to do a good job, and if he failed, then woe betide him.

At least the folk here were free to come and go as they pleased. Flora led them to a tree in the corner. 'We'll settle down here as at least we'll have a little shelter should it rain during the night,' she said, then looking at Archie carried on, 'We'll have Duke to protect us so don't go worrying. We are well away from that brute back at the pub because if we'd have stayed we could only have expected far worse to come!'

Archie noticed that Flora's voice had changed from a soft defeated tune to a stronger, fight the devil one, and he was glad of it too.

He knew he was too young to fully understand what happened the night when she got out of bed crying, yet Bill'd had a big smile on his face next day as if he was happy with what had occurred. Nor did he understand why that stranger he'd clonked on the head had been grappling with Flora in the tap room in the dark! Didn't make much sense to him. All he understood was that there was something badly wrong with it all.

Then he remembered the book. 'I brought this for you,' he said, handing Flora her book of stories.

'Oh, Archie!' She hugged him to her and he felt her shoulders heave as she began to cry.

'I'm sorry, I didn't mean to upset you?'

She held him at arms' length. 'You haven't, I'm crying because I'm so happy. I never thought to take the book with me as we were in a rush to get out of there, but you did, Archie. That was ever so thoughtful.'

He smiled, knowing that he'd pleased her and that meant a lot to him.

They huddled together with Duke curled up nearby but he could tell the dog was on high alert should anyone dare get close to them. The last thing he remembered before falling asleep was the sound of Flora's voice as she soothed Bobby to sleep as she sang him a lullaby.

***

'Can't understand it meself', Cook said, looking at Polly as she paused a moment, both hands buried in a bowl of pastry which was almost ready to be dropped on the floured counter and rolled out with a gigantic wooden pin. Even making a simple apple pie reminded her of Archie.

'What?' Polly blinked with frustration.

'It's not "what" it's "pardon"...' Cook said acerbically. 'I mean how the police have a big clue now that Archie might be with your uncle, but can't find any trace of the man.'

Polly harrumphed. 'How many master sweeps do you think there are in the area, Mrs Stockley? There are so many and they all look so alike under a thick coating of soot!' She scoffed, causing Cook to wrinkle her nose in disgust.

Polly could be a haughty little madam at times and she was beginning to wonder if the girl knew more than she was letting on.

Polly began drying the dishes and no more was said until the pie had been prepared and popped in the oven.

'Fancy a cup of tea, Mrs Stockley?' she offered.

Cook's features softened, her blue eyes twinkling. 'Aye, go on then. Look, I didn't mean to imply anything, I'm just frustrated the lad hasn't been found yet.'

Polly nodded, then went to fill the large well-used kettle, settling it to boil on the hearth. 'Honestly, I have no more clue where Archie is than you have. Trouble is my Uncle Bill has fallen out with most of the family, so they don't keep in touch.'

Cook narrowed her eyes. 'And why might that be?'

Polly swallowed. 'He nearly beat my Uncle Jim, that's his brother, to death over some money what was owed to him. I don't know the ins and outs of it all but it was a very nasty business. Uncle Jim is lucky to be alive.'

'Then why do you bother yourself with such a man?' It was a fair question Cook thought but she had no idea how the girl would respond.

There was a long, protracted silence. Then Polly let out a breath. 'Because me Auntie Sonia, who I was close to, asked me to keep an eye on him, she asked me on her deathbed and all. He was different before she died. When she was alive he was so happy. They had a good marriage, something a lot of folk envied and they planned to start a family, but it wasn't to be…' her voice trailed off and her face took a faraway look.

'But then?'

She shook her head sadly. 'Then he went completely off the rails after she passed over. Lost interest in life itself, began drinking and gambling and all the things that went with that lifestyle.'

Cook quirked a brow. 'How'd you mean?'

Polly lowered her voice to barely a whisper. 'Picking up floosies. Though the one he's knocking around with now is very nice, but even she can't tame him. It's like something inside him died when my Auntie Sonia left this earth.'

Cook clucked her teeth and nodded. 'One can never tell with folk, it must have been hard for him, for sure. But most people don't go around trying to kill their own flesh and blood because they've lost someone!'

Polly appeared to mull it over for a moment before saying, 'You're probably right. I'm going home for a visit in a day or two. I can't promise but if I hear anything from my family about my uncle's whereabouts, I'll let the police know, but it's very doubtful.'

Cook nodded. Polly was a good girl really, even if she'd put family loyalty before the dire need to find Archie. Well at least now she was prepared to do something about it. Whether anything would come of it, would be another thing, of course.

***

Archie awoke with a start, his heart pounding. Where was he? The cold was nipping at his fingers and toes and his back ached something chronic.

'Sssh, Archie, go back to sleep,' Flora soothed. But it was too late, he was wide awake and it was beginning to get light, birds were starting to sing as though they were set for the day ahead and looking forward to it. Though the same couldn't be said for the folk waking in Itchy Park. He noticed a few people were bundling their belongings together as if getting prepared to move on, and who knew, maybe it would be the police who would throw them out of this place. The wealthy in the area didn't like to see the down and outs. They were a constant reminder of things they didn't want to worry about. A bad smell beneath their noses. What was it Mr Dickens had said in his book *A Christmas Carol* about the poor and destitute when he spoke of them dying? *They had better do it, and decrease the surplus population?*

'We'd better get a shift on,' Flora said stoically.

Archie glanced across the semi-darkness to see a man and woman beneath another tree and he wondered what they were up to. The woman's garish clothing seemed to be in a state of disarray and the man was pawing at her. It reminded him of the goings-on in the tap room at the pub last night.

Before Archie could question it, Flora said, 'Come along, let's get out of here before the police arrive.'

Bobby got the directions to the big house muddled up. In his mind, it was in a nearby street, but in reality, it was further away, but when all seemed lost, he pointed at a house which had a gleaming brass plaque beside the door. 'That's it!' he said, his voice sounding excitable and Archie realised he was right, he recognised it too.

'You're right, Nipper,' he said. 'I remember that fancy gaslight outside in the street and those lovely flowers on the windowsill.'

Pleased to have found the place, Flora said, 'How would we find the tradesman's entrance?'

'Around the back,' said Archie. 'But if we take those steps here at the front, they lead down to the kitchen. I think we'd stand more chance of speaking to someone.' He guessed the cook would be busy right now, preparing breakfasts for those upstairs just like Cook would back at his uncle's house.

A vision of the kind-hearted, rosy-cheeked woman with the wide smile that melted his heart came to mind, then faded away as Flora spoke.

'You three stay here and I'll knock the door!'

'Take Bobby with you,' Archie urged. He knew that cherubic face and blond hair would elicit sympathy and they'd probably also recognise him from his last visit to the house with Bill. If that didn't tear at the heartstrings nothing would.

Chapter Nine

Bill woke and groaning loudly, clutched his head, he'd drank too much last night, but one of Flora's special breakfasts would soon sort him out. Thick bacon with fried eggs and fried bread, that should do the trick. Oh, and a nice cup of strong sweet tea.

'Woman!' he cried out. But there was no answer. That was odd, the place sounded empty almost. There was no noise of the boys rolling their marbles in the corner or bickering between themselves, no sounds of Flora raking the ashes in the grate or pottering around the place humming softly to herself. Roughly, he pulled back the curtain from around the bed with so much force he almost pulled the rail down on top of himself.

There was no one there at all. 'Duke!' he called out.

Where the hell were they? He just bet the bitch had gone downstairs to talk the landlady into giving her a job…then it all came back at him full force. He remembered now. He owed someone some payment for his gambling debts and the man had come after him last night while he was out with Flora, he did the only thing he knew how, to offer her up as payment to him. It sickened him to the stomach to imagine the pair of them together, but that would have been his debts cleared, well that time and maybe a few times more. Otherwise, he could end up in a debtors prison, or worse, beaten up lying half-dead in the gutter. It was a choice he'd had to make. She wasn't pleased about it, but he'd persuaded her it would only be the once and he didn't tell her all she was expected to do for the man either, else she'd never have gone along with it in the first place. But he'd held the trump card by telling her if she didn't keep the man company and be nice to him, she'd never see her precious Bobby ever again.

He got out of bed fully clothed and called Flora's name from the landing, causing a woman from the next room to poke her head out of the door. 'Piss off, you nosy old cow!' he barked at her, causing her to retreat inside.

Then he had an idea, Connie would know where she was, she'd have seen her leaving. But when he got downstairs to see the woman polishing the wooden bar top, she shook her head. 'No, sorry, Bill. I ain't seen her for days, thought you usually kept her cooped up.'

He scowled. Now he was in an evil mood and someone would pay for it if they all didn't show up soon. He thumped the wall, hardly noticing he'd skinned his knuckles and drawn blood.

**

Archie clung on to Duke's makeshift lead which was really a piece of frayed cord, as he peered through the black wrought iron railings to watch the door open down below to Flora and Bobby. He couldn't make out who the person was who was speaking to Flora through the half-open door, but now it was opening fully and Flora and Bobby were stepping inside.

It seemed an age while they were inside the house, and all the while, Archie had to blow on his hands to keep them warm. Duke didn't seem to mind too much. His ears had cocked up when he'd noticed a black cat at the property next door. Archie felt a sudden yank on the cord and he had to fight to hold the dog back from chasing the cat.

So many people passed by in the street considering it was early morning. He even noticed some deliveries to the house itself. A boy dressed in a white tunic and matching trousers and sporting a peaked cap on his head, delivered a large cloth-covered tray to the house. He guessed there were probably some sort of pastries beneath the cloth, and behind him, an older man carrying a wooden crate of bread on his head, walked down the basement steps below. Even though the loaves were wrapped in muslin cloths, he knew what they were by the delicious smell wafting his way. It made his tummy growl with hunger. He'd been tempted to whip something off the young lad's tray as he descended the steps to the kitchen entrance, but the fight with his conscience told him it was wrong.

Finally, after seeing the boy, and two other delivery men come and go, Bobby appeared at the top of the steps, his green eyes all shiny and bright as if he was excited about something.

'Ma's got herself a job here!' he declared proudly, 'And I can stay an' all.' Then his face clouded over, 'But there's only room for one lad though…' he looked down at his feet as if he was upset they couldn't take Archie with them and couldn't bear to look him in the eye while he imparted the news. 'And they definitely will not take Duke either.'

Archie looked on sadly, what could he and Duke do now?

'Don't worry none,' he said, trying to sound bright and cheerful, then he patted Bobby's shoulder as a sign of reassurance. 'I'll take Duke to try to find my old neighbour, Ginny. She'll help get me back to my uncle and Duke can have a home there too, and you can visit whenever you like!'

'Really?' Bobby met his gaze and blinked.

'Yes, really, Nipper.'

'Oh, I forgot to tell you, you're to come down to the kitchen before you go. Ma has talked that Edna one into giving you some breakfast and she says she can give Duke some scraps an' all.'

'That's really kind of her.' Archie had no idea how he was going to find Ginny but it was the only plan he had for time being.

After relishing every mouthful of porridge and a couple of rounds of toast with a cup of tea, with full bellies, Archie and Duke said farewell to Flora and Bobby. Flora clutched him to her chest. 'Archie, if you can't find nowhere to go, come back here and I'll ask again for you.' Archie knew the young woman meant well, but he could see there was no place for him here. Flora had fallen in lucky to get a job as a maid of all work as one was due to leave the following week as she was getting married and she could show her the ropes before she left.

'Bye, Archie,' Bobby said, as he wiped away a tear.

'So long, Nipper,' Archie ruffled his hair playfully. 'Maybe we'll meet again someday!' He left before he broke down himself, he was a big boy now and he was going to take care of himself and Duke too.

'Well, Duke,' he said, as he climbed the basement steps and arrived up onto the street above, 'it's only me and you now, mate. Which direction shall we take?' Duke looked up at him with big soulful eyes. Archie took a deep breath and turned right.

***

Archie felt like he'd been walking for hours on end but it couldn't have been all that long as he noticed the clock on the church at the end of the road he now found himself on, displayed, half past eight. It was still early on and he had no clue where his old street was so he could find Ginny. He figured if he asked someone where the docks were he'd soon find it.

He'd asked a few people in passing if they knew where Dock Street was but they seemed as baffled as he was. Most seemed to be rushing as if a boy and his dog didn't warrant their time or attention. But still, he tried to keep his hopes up.

By early afternoon, he was starving again and he hoped it wouldn't rain as then he'd have to find shelter.

As he passed a pub called "The Butcher's Arms" a man walked out, swaying like he was drunk as he crab-walked from one side to the other. The man paused, and then looked him up and down, his eyes seemed to focus on the pair of them, as he said, 'That's a mighty fine dog, you've got there, sonny? Want to sh…shell him?'

'No, sir,' he replied, holding on tightly to Duke's lead.

'Shhhhh…shame,' said the man and then he hiccupped loudly. There was a lot of raucous noise coming from inside the pub, shouts, yells and laughter, and Archie feared being seen in case Bill was inside. It looked like his kind of place. He hoped the man would never find Flora and Bobby ever again.

Hope was starting to fade for Archie by mid-afternoon. He'd been walking around for some time and now his feet ached and he so wished his ma was still alive to find him and take him home to the little humble house they'd lived in. How had it all come to this?

'Cor! That's a big dog!'

Archie turned to see a lad behind him, not much bigger than himself, with his hands dug deep in his pockets. He stared at the boy whose clothes were all tattered and torn. His face smeared with dirt. He seemed friendly enough.

'Yes, he's the biggest dog I've ever seen.' Archie patted Duke and drew him nearer in case the boy tried to take him away.

The lad let out a long whistle. 'Bet he's worth a bob or two!'

'Well, he's not for sale to you nor anyone else!' Archie said crossly, pulling Duke even closer to himself.

'Keer yer 'air on, mate! I was only saying, like.'

'Do you know where Dock Street is?'

The boy shook his head. 'Should I? Why?'

'I used to live there, see, I want to go back home to find a lady I know.'

'Well just 'cos I don't know it, doesn't mean someone else wouldn't. I knows a very clever old gent what might be able to help. He might even 'ave a job for the likes of you. He's a charitable sort of fella!'

'As long as it's not going up chimneys, I've had enough of that caper,' Archie groaned.

'Oh no, me ol' son, this is much better than that! He wouldn't make you a climbing boy.' The boy's eyes lit up. 'In fact, yer don't 'ave to do very much at all!'

This all sounded too good to be true to Archie. He narrowed his gaze. 'Are you trying to trick me to get hold of my dog?'

'No, I swear, cross me heart and 'ope to die.' He made the sign of the cross over his chest and cocked a grin.

What else could he do? He had little option other than to carry on walking the streets for hours and then he still might not find Ginny.

'All right,' Archie sighed, 'show us the way. What's your name by the way?'

'Smithy.'

What kind of a name was that?

'Smithy, what?'

'Don't rightly know, I'm just always known by that name. I lost me Ma and Pa when I was very young, but Casper, he's the old gent what I just told you about, he took me in and helped me when I had no one else. Otherwise, it would be the workhouse for the likes o' me.'

Archie nodded with understanding. 'I lost my own mother recently, and I never knew a father either, so I guess that makes me an orphan like you.'

Smithy laid his hand on Archie's shoulder. 'I guess you could say we are like brothers then. I tell you what, as neither of us 'as any family to call our own…' his eyes widened, 'let's be blood brothers!'

Archie screwed up his face. 'What do you mean?'

'I saw some boys do it once. They pricked their fingers with a pin and then held their fingers together so their blood mingled and said now they was blood brothers.'

Archie didn't much like the thought of pricking his finger, it could hurt. And he hated the sight of blood, so he said, 'I reckon we could just say we are brothers, anyhow. What do you think?'

'I fink I like that idea,' Smithy said. 'Can I hold the dog's lead?'

For a moment, Archie feared the lad was going to trick him and run off with Duke but, knowing how strong the dog was and how he liked Archie, he decided to hand the lad the cord, which he took with a big smile on his face. 'Thank you,' he beamed. Archie could tell how much this meant to him and he liked the idea of having a brother as he'd never had one before in all of his life.

***

When Polly arrived back at the big house she was just about to tell Cook that no one had set eyes on her Uncle Bill, when Cook blurted out. 'You never guess what, Poll, the police managed to track down your uncle!'

Polly blinked. 'Never to goodness! I was just about to tell you none of the family have seen hide nor hair of him. How come?'

'Apparently, he'd scammed a few people and someone knew where he was residing, above a pub called "The Horse and Hounds".'

'That's great!' Her eyes scanned the kitchen as if Archie might somehow be present at the house. 'Where is he then?'

Cook shook her head, her eyes welling up. 'Sorry to have to tell you but Archie's not here, he hasn't been found as yet.'

'Are the police holding him then for some reason?'

'No, they don't know where he is. Your uncle claims his girlfriend, Flora, left with the kids and the dog and he denies all knowledge of where they could have gone to. Seems to me as if he might be telling the truth about that.'

'Oh no,' Polly said, her hands flying to her face. 'I don't know Flora all that well, I hope she takes care of the boy. She has a young son called, Bobby, the little boy who cleaned the chimneys here.'

Cook nodded with understanding. 'Here's what I think, Poll, and you have to face facts. My guess is Flora left for a good reason and maybe the boys are safer with her rather than your uncle!' It was too late, Cook had said what had been on her mind all this time.

Polly's eyes flashed. 'My uncle isn't all bad you know, Mrs Stockley!' She stomped out of the kitchen, slamming the door behind her almost taking it off its hinges, leaving Cook in a quandry. She couldn't afford to upset the girl as she needed her help in the kitchen. Maybe she'd just as well give her time to calm down, she'd leave peeling the spuds until later when Polly had cooled right down. She could have kicked herself for speaking her thoughts out loud and should have thought better of it, but all this time her heart had broken thinking about Archie and being in the clutches of that man. So if he'd managed to somehow get away, then good for him!

***

'Now when you see's Casper, don't say nuffink!' Smithy advised. 'He's a shrewd old geezer, let him look you over first. That way you stand more chance of being taken on.'

'Taken on to do what?'

'Look, let's see if he finks you can be one of us first off.'

Smithy led Archie along a dark alleyway which opened up into a courtyard with whitewashed walls. The place smelled strongly of dung and there was straw scattered everywhere underfoot. A couple of large black cartwheels were strung on one of the walls as if for decoration and directly opposite that wall were a couple of stables, and straight ahead was a cobbled area which led through to an ornate archway, which Archie guessed was an entrance of sorts. And directly in front of him was the back of some sort of pub, which was painted black and white and looked Elizabethan in style.

'What kind of place is this?' Archie asked.

Smithy grinned. 'This, my dear, is a coaching house! A place where genteel folk rest their horses whilst they either sup at the inn or they might even stay here!' He embellished the fact with a flourish of his hand, and then bowed, causing Archie to break into a fit of giggles. 'That archway over there is where the coaches come in. They get guests staying here overnight sometimes and mail coaches pass through here, too.'

'Does this Mr Casper, live here in one of the stables?'

'No. Look, you're going to find out soon enough…'

Archie noticed an elderly man walking towards them. 'Is this him?' He asked nervously.

'Yes. Remember what I said, don't speak first.'

As the man approached, Archie noticed his strange shuffling gait. His bald head shone and he wore his long double-breasted coat over a pair of breeches, it looked as though it had seen better days, but had once been a nice velvet trimmed coat. He wondered how he had acquired it.

'So, then, Smithy, who have we here?' Casper asked, with a twinkle in his grey-blue eyes, that told Archie he was warm and friendly. His long peppered white beard kept drawing Archie's eyes, he'd never seen anything like it before. For what was missing off the old man's head was made up for in that beard.

'This here is Master Archibald Ledbetter. An orphan of the parish who badly needs a job, I fought we could find him somefink, here, Mr Casper.'

Casper stood studying Archie for a moment as he scratched his chin. 'I dare say we can find you something, young man. A stable boy like Smithy, maybe? But I can't afford to pay you, though you'll have a roof over your head and plenty of vitals from the inn.'

'Thank you, sir,' Archie said, 'but what about Duke?'

'Who is this duke you speak of? I didn't know we had any royalty here?' Casper threw back his head and laughed at his own joke. 'You mean the dog, I assume?'

'Yes, sir.'

'I dare say we can find a job for him as a ratter or something. Smithy, take Archibald to his lodgings and get some tucker for him and the dog.' Casper lowered his voice as he whispered something in Smithy's ear. Smithy just nodded and smiled, but it made Archie feel uncomfortable not knowing what was being said.

'It's all right,' Smithy said when he could see Archie's face. 'He just told me you and the dog are to sleep with me in the stable. It's 'orright in there really, keeps us warm and dry with all the hay but sometimes, especially in summer, it don't 'alf pong to high heaven though! We 'ave to be careful with any naked flames in there mind as there are bales of hay which could go up in no time at all. I usually use a lantern but make sure it's well snuffed out when I got to sleep or go out anywhere.'

'It's fine,' said Archie. 'The street where I used to live stank sometimes as well as we lived near the tannery and the knackers' yard.'

After Smithy had shown him where he could bed down for the night, the boy led him across the cobbled courtyard to a door that opened on both the top and the bottom, it was like two doors in one, with the smallest on top. Archie had never seen one like it before except at the stables.

Puzzled, he watched as Smithy, who was whistling to himself, rapped on the door. The top half opened to reveal a middle-aged woman with oily looking skin and a mobcap on top of her salt and peppered hair, who was smiling down on them.

'This 'ere is Cassie. Cassie, this is Archie. Old Casper's taking him on to help wiv the horses.'

'So, he's going to be an ostler, is he?' she tapped her nose with her index finger and threw back her head and laughed.

Archie noticed an exchange of glances between the pair and he briefly wondered what it was about. It reminded him of when Casper had whispered in Smithy's ear earlier, making him feel excluded, somehow.

'Nice to meet yer, Archie,' Cassie said when the merriment had faded away, making him briefly forget his concerns. 'Now, I'm the cook at this 'ere establishment, so if you need anything just tap at the door as I can get you the scraps orf the tables inside. We have some fine gentlemen, nobs like,' she sniffed, 'what dine here and what don't care if they leave morsels of food behind after spending good money. They've got lots of money to burn in their very deep pockets!' She sighed deeply. 'The rest of us mere mortals 'ave to make do and mend.'

Archie nodded, totally understanding what she meant. He'd noticed his own uncle often left food on his plate that his own ma would have thought sacrilege to leave behind. *Waste not want not.* How could Ma though have been born into that sort of lifestyle yet ended up so poor? It was all a mystery to him.

'What yer got for us today, Cass?'

Her grin was so wide it displayed her front teeth which were black and rotting away.

'I managed to squirrel away a couple o'slices of meat pie and a few tatas for yer. I've kept 'em warm for you, ducks! There's enough to share with Archie and I've got some gravy to go along with it.'

'We better have 'em now then as we might get busy later when the horses arrive,' Smithy laughed. 'I need to show the new boy the ropes!' He slapped Archie so hard on his back that he almost toppled over and had to fight to remain upstanding. 'What's the matter with yer?'

'Duke!' Archie said, 'He hasn't eaten for ages either.'

Smithy turned and called out to the woman. 'Cassie, do you have anything for the mutt, 'ere?'

Cassie looked at them both. 'I got a nice bit of ham bone, used it in a stew earlier, still got a bit o' meat on the bone as well.'

Archie grinned. 'Thanks, missus!' He couldn't believe how lucky he was to have landed on his feet. Soon he'd find his way home. He'd ask as many coach drivers as possible who came to the inn if they knew Uncle Walter or his old neighbour Ginny. The trouble was he didn't know how to explain the addresses to them. Were there a lot of Dock Streets around, he wondered? All he could say about his uncle's house was that it was a large house in the country, what use was that? Would people believe him anyhow? The clothing he wore hardly made him look like a member of the gentry, did it?

Cassie handed the boys a steaming tin dish each slathered in thick gravy, the aroma made Archie's stomach growl with hunger, Smithy had put the bone for Duke in his pocket. 'Now watch no one at the inn sees you eating that lot, lads, it's more than me job's worth, you're supposed to pay for your grub 'ere even though you're working in the stables.'

Smithy cocked her a grin. 'I know how to keep things quiet,' he said. He turned to Archie, 'We don't want to lose the chance of all this free grub, so you keep quiet an' all, right?'

'Of course!' It went without saying, who was he going to tell anyhow? He followed Smithy back to the stables where they sat on a hay bale each and polished off the pie and potatoes, shovelling big chunks into their mouths, as Duke sat happily in the corner nibbling at the ham bone. My, the food was so tasty and Duke was enjoying his bone too by the look of it.

After they'd eaten their fill, Archie felt like falling asleep as his belly was so full, he'd had little sleep after being disturbed in the middle of the night and then trying to kip with one eye open at Itchy Park in amongst the letches and the beggars.

Smithy stood and said, 'Another five minutes and then we'll have to work for Mr Casper.'

'I'm fine with that, but what do you want me to do?'

'He says there's a couple of coaches heading this way later, we're to feed and stable the horses for the night. Rich pickings there an' all.'

Archie blinked. 'Rich pickings?'

'Yes, those rich folk leave stuff hanging around when they stop at the inn, they're so tired and drink too much alcohol. Casper waits until the time is right and then sends us in to pick their pockets, or if we're really lucky, sometimes we can get into their rooms and out again without them even noticing.'

'But that's stealing!' Archie was shocked.

'And this is life, Archie, me old son! They got too much anyhow, more than they can spend!' He pushed back the brim of his cap and grinned, and for the first time, something began to dawn on Archie.

'But I thought this was just a stable boy job!'

'My, my, someone's lead a sheltered life...' Smithy sat beside Archie. 'You're green as grass, ain't yer? Look, this is a big opportunity for you. Do all right by old Casper and he'll do all right by you. It's better than walking the streets with an empty belly and no bed for the night, you'd be at the mercy of all sorts out there.'

Archie decided the boy was right, but he didn't like the sound of it at all. No wonder Mr Casper and Cassie had been acting oddly with Smithy, they were all in on it together and he'd just been lured into a den of thieves!

Chapter Ten

It was back-breaking work sorting out the horses for the night and having to muck out the stables and clean inside and outside the coaches too. Duke watched on from a distance and to Archie's surprise, the dog sorted out a few rats that were scurrying around the courtyard by barking at them and frightening them away, just as Mr Casper arrived on the scene. This time his head was covered as he wore a big wideawake hat and appeared more dressed up than he had previously in the day.

'I thought that dog would make a good ratter when I first saw him,' he said, with a big smile on his face. 'How are you settling in here, Archie? Not working you too hard, are we?' He studied Archie's face for confirmation.

Archie shook his head. 'No, not at all, Mr Casper.' Archie lied for fear the old man might send him away, but he was dead on his feet. His legs were aching and his eyes felt like lead, but he appreciated it was far better than climbing any chimney.

'Good, now then…I have a little job for you later. When the church bell chimes ten tonight, I want you to go into the inn through that door there!' He pointed to the same door where Cassie had given them the food. 'Now, the kitchen door shall be left open for you. Go into the bar room and start collecting the empties. I have an arrangement with the landlord.' He lowered his voice to barely a whisper. 'There'll be plenty of customers there who are under the influence…'

'The influence of what, sir?'

'Why, alcohol of course!' Casper rubbed the palms of his hands together and smiled surreptitiously. 'Most of them rich sorts won't have their wits about them. Check to see if you notice any who have their wallets on show, bulging from their pockets or if they've placed them down on the table beside them. Anything you notice that might be of interest. If any of their sort drop coins on the floor, help to pick them up and pocket some. Not so many as they'd notice, mind!'

'You want me to s…steal from them, sir?'

'No, not tonight. It's your first time, I want to you find Smithy, he'll go in and make a clean sweep, you watch what he does but also watch that no one notices, if they do, for heaven's sake warn him as soon as possible, got it?'

'I think so, sir.'

Casper patted Archie's head. 'Good lad. Now get on with your work and wait until the clock chimes ten. There'll be something in it for you.'

Archie worked solidly, somehow he'd managed to acquire a second wind. One, two, three…the church clock was chiming, he carried on counting. Ten chimes, then no more. He looked at Smithy, who was busy washing down a mud-splattered coach with a soapy rag. 'Well, go on then,' he urged. 'You know what you have to do. I won't have time to come with you after all…'

'But Mr Casper said as it's my first time I was to check out the bar for any signs of wallets bulging from the customers' pockets and then send for you!'

'Aw look, Archie, you need to throw yerself in the deep end, don't listen to what Casper says, one of us has to finish up 'ere, if we both go in we'll get noticed anyhow.'

Archie swallowed. How he wished he was back at his uncle's lovely home snuggled down in his own comfy feather bed with Cook and Polly fussing over him, and Mr Featherstone allowing him to help out in the orchard. All of that seemed a million years ago. His stomach was doing somersaults as he fought to cope with the feeling of nausea at what he was about to do.

He headed over to the double stable-like door, noticing it was slightly ajar. There were a couple of oil lamps lit on the wooden counters but there was no one there. Lots of dirty pots, pans and dishes lay about in a higgledy-piggledy fashion as if waiting to be washed. In the distance, he heard the sound of raucous laughter and voices, and the odd glass being clinked. Slowly, he made his way in the direction of the noise, unaware of what awaited him.

***

'I'm telling you, I won't be right until I've tracked my nephew down!' Cook heard the master say through the drawing-room door. 'He's at the mercy of all and sundry whilst he's away from this house. In any case, I promised my sister on her deathbed I'd take care of the boy, even though I'm not much good at relating to young boys.'

Cook could hear the sound of another male present in the room.

'But the boy shouldn't be your responsibility, Walter. At least not whilst his half-brother is still alive!'

Cook shuddered involuntarily. His brother? So Walter must have known who Archie's father was. What a scandal it had been at the time, him being a married man and old enough to be Alicia's father and all. Then her giving birth to twin boys, one who died hours after birth and was buried in the grounds here in an unmarked grave, and the other who entered a life of poverty in the East End of London.

Oh, she'd brought shame on the household all right. Her parents had never fully recovered from the shock of it all, especially as the children's father had been a friend of Sir Ronald's. Secretly, Cook had thought that what had happened had sent both Sir Ronald and Lady Emily to an early grave and maybe Archie's real father along with them.

Cook moved away from the door as she could hear the voices drawing nearer but stepping back, she bumped into Polly.

'Hey gerroff my foot!' Polly squealed.

'Sorry,' Cook whispered. 'Let's return to the kitchen, they're coming out.'

Polly frowned but did as Cook ordered, and later when they were both settled with a cup of tea, Cook explained the whole story to the girl.

'Well, I never,' Polly said, her mouth agape for a few seconds. 'I have wondered what that grave was in the grounds. It doesn't give the baby's name just that a young soul has gone to heaven and the date of his passing.'

Cook nodded. 'There was too much shame attached to it all. The Brookings didn't want people to know. It was an awful time here as there was a lot of tension in the house, then when Walter's parents, Sir

Ronald and Lady Emily Brooking, passed away a couple of years later, he inherited everything, when really Alicia being the eldest of all should have been entitled to something. But no doubt she was written out of the will due to circumstance.'

'The poor girl. So that baby that died would have been Archie's twin brother?'

'Yes. You have to promise me if I tell you something you are not to tell another living soul, Poll.' She was trusting the young woman to keep her trap shut. Cook had kept it a secret for so many years, but she felt she had to tell someone.

Polly sat there wide-eyed in expectation. 'I promise on me life, Mrs Stockley, I do.'

Cook drew a breath. 'I just overheard a conversation with someone and the master where they spoke about Archie's halfbrother!'

'Never to goodness! Do you know who he is?'

Cook nodded slowly. 'He's the son of Sir Richard Pomfrey, a wealthy landowner in the area. I expect you've heard of him? He passed away some time ago.'

Polly shook her head. 'Can't say as I do…' Her mind was obviously working overtime. 'Hang on, does he have a son called, William who's in charge of the estate these days? A handsome young brute and all.'

'The very one and the same. You might have read about him in the newspaper. He's been here a couple of times on business with Walter.'

Polly looked up at the ceiling as if deep in thought. 'You know what this means?'

'No?'

'It means that young Archie could be the heir to a fortune and that he also has a brother!'

'Sssh,' scolded Cook. 'Walls have ears, I don't want Mrs Linley or Mr Simpkins getting wind of this. But perhaps you're right. Though I don't think we should mention it ever again. Just because the master has acknowledged this, it doesn't mean that Richard Pomfrey did nor his son.'

Polly nodded, but Cook could tell the young woman's mind was racing to catch up with it all. She had no idea that Walter even realised he was somehow related to William, though not by blood.

Secrets had a way of getting out though and Huntingdon Hall held more secrets than most.

***

No one batted an eyelid as Archie entered the bar room of the coaching inn. The landlord was in the midst of handing out a couple of foaming tankards to a barmaid, and none of the male customers paid any attention to his presence. The landlord, then stopped what he was doing and looking at Archie, winked at him, as if to say all was fine. That settled Archie's stomach for him. They all seemed to be in on it, those that worked here: Smithy, Mr Casper, Cassie, the landlord, he expected even the barmaid and all! It didn't make it right though, not by a long chalk, but he tried to reassure himself that a lot of the customers were well off sorts who could afford to miss a few bob here and there. Besides if he didn't do what was asked of him, both he and Duke could well find themselves wandering the streets once again.

His eyes darted around the room, but he could see no unattended bulging leather wallets anywhere like

Mr Casper had mentioned, but then his eyes were drawn to something silver and shiny on a small wooden table in the corner. It was some sort of snuff box, just like he'd seen in the glass cabinet at that big house where he went up the chimney. He drew nearer and could see it was oval in shape and had a lady and gentleman engraved into it. The gentleman who it appeared to belong to was in deep conversation with someone else. How could he lift it off the table without being seen? Thinking for a moment, he pretended to drop something on the floor so that he was on his hands and knees beneath the table, then his hand shot up and snatched it so fast that no one appeared to have noticed, quickly he stuffed it into his jacket pocket. Then stood.

'You there, boy!' someone said. Oh, no, he must have been seen, he began to quiver all over, his mouth dry as a bone. 'Go and get me a jug of porter from the bar!'

It was one of the men seated at the next table, so he hadn't been viewed after all. Relief flooded through him. The man had big bushy sideburns and a silver-tipped cane by his side. He was obviously someone of fine breeding, Archie could tell by his well-tailored clothes.

'Go on, lad, there'll be a sixpence in it for you!' The man urged.

He smiled. 'Thank you, sir,' as the man's hand dipped into his pocket and gave him some coinage.

As Archie waited to be served by the bar, the landlord winked at him again. 'Well done, son, yer a natural!' He handed Archie the earthenware jug of porter. 'Mind how you go, watch you don't spill nothing.' Archie nodded, and when he arrived at the table was rewarded with a shiny silver sixpence for his good deed but he did feel bad about whipping the snuff-box. But yet again those two men at the next table were so busy putting the world to rights that the owner of the silver box hadn't even noticed! How fickle some of these rich folk were in their well-fitted garb with velvet collars and silk cravats, whilst half of London was starving and fortunate indeed to have clothing on their backs, shoes on their feet and a bed for the night. So many of the poor suffered. But then he felt bad for thinking that way as Uncle Walter was rich.

Before he had a chance to think any more of it, he noticed a man stood by the bar with a thick leather wallet poking out of his jacket pocket. How could he slip that away? It was getting busy by the bar, so Archie pretended to bump into him.

'You clumsy young oaf!' The man was furious as he clipped Archie around the earhole, so hard it stung and he reeled backwards as his hands flew instinctively to his head. No one in the bar room seemed to care he had been attacked by the man. Served the brute right that now he had lifted his wallet, which was safe down the back of his kegs. Realising he had better get out of there as attention might be drawn to him, he walked out of the warm room and into the cold courtyard outside.

As soon as Smithy caught sight of him, he hurried him along to the stables where he put his finger to his mouth and whispered. 'We need to take care, so no one knows what's going on, did yer manage to nab anyfink?'

Archie nodded breathlessly. Although he knew what he'd done was morally wrong, nevertheless, he felt a frisson of excitement course his veins. He turned out his pockets to display the silver snuff box and the leather wallet.

'Cor! Archie, me old son. You've done very well for a first timer, very well indeed!' Smithy blinked several times in surprise, then patted him on the back.

'I caught a right wallop off the gent I bumped into, but I did manage to nab his wallet!' Archie said with great aplomb.

Smithy grinned. 'Serves the codger right! Got more money than sense, half these la-de-da sorts! Now, let's see how much is in the wallet!' He snatched it from Archie's outstretched hand and leafed through it. 'Whoah! I ain't never seen so much money in all me born days.'

Archie stared in amazement. 'Do you think we should keep all of that? The man will notice soon it's gone and might guess it was me.'

'I dunno, we better ask old Casper. It's a darn sight more than we'd normally get away with. He extracted a couple of gold sovereigns out of the purse section and handed one to Archie and kept one for himself. 'We won't show Casper we got these, he doesn't give us much of the spoils anyhow, but we'd better take the snuff-box and wallet to him right away!'

Archie said nothing of the sixpence in his pocket, he'd earned it fair and square so classed it as his own. Something told him to keep quiet about that.

'Come on then!' Smithy urged as if time was of the essence.

Archie followed him out of the stables and up a wrought iron staircase at the back of the inn which led to a small door. Smithy rapped three times.

'Who is it?' Casper asked from behind the locked door.

'Smithy.'

'What's the password?'

'London.' He turned to Archie, 'I go through this caper every time, but when we're allowed in you'll see why.'

The door opened a fraction as the boys were allowed access to the room. Archie's eyes nearly popped out of his head. It was like a real treasure trove of a place where there were paintings in gilt frames, lots of styles of ornaments, shelves full of books and boxes and, sat at a desk brimming over with dusty looking files and ledgers, was Casper himself—appearing smaller than usual in amongst all the spoils. He smiled when he saw both boys and smoothed down his beard as if in expectation.

'So, what have you brought for me then, young Archie?' He wore fingerless gloves and rubbed his hands together in anticipation as he licked his lips.

Smithy cleared his throat. 'A silver snuff-box and a wallet of money I managed to procure with Archie's assistance, Mr Casper.'

Archie glared at Smithy, he was making it sound as if he had got those things away all by himself.

Casper's eyes grew large. 'Let's be having them then.'

Archie placed the snuff-box on the desk in front of the man, whilst Smithy produced the wallet from the back pocket of his trousers.

Casper smiled and then his smile faded as quickly as it had arrived. 'You look troubled, lad. Is anything wrong?' He stared at Archie over his top of gold-rimmed specs.

'There's a lot of money in the wallet, sir, I was thinking maybe we ought to just take some money from it and put it back in the gent's pocket.'

Casper threw back his head and laughed. He paused a moment and then looking at Smithy said, 'Do you hear this, Smithy? The boy here says we should return the money to the very nice gentleman!'

Smithy began to laugh along with the old man as if making Archie out to be a figure of fun, but deep down Archie realised that the lad was scared of Casper and would go along with anything he said.

Casper's face took on a more serious expression as he said, 'Look, seeing as how I'm a nice kind, benevolent *gentleman* myself, I'll slip you a couple of shillings for your time, dears!' He said, opening the purse pocket of the wallet and handing one shilling to Archie and another to Smithy. Then he lifted a large magnifying glass that was on top of one of the ledgers beside him and holding it up to his right eye so that it looked enormous to Archie, he studied the snuff box. 'Quality stuff!' he exclaimed with a note of excitement in his voice. 'This ain't your Petticoat Lane Market flotsam and jetsam! It's proper hallmarked silver, sold from a reputable silversmith's shop by the look of it. You've done well, boys.' He stroked his beard as if mulling things over as both boys stood staring at him in wonder. Finally, he placed the magnifying glass on the ledger and breaking the long silence said, 'Now the two of you keep schtum about this, understood?' Both nodded, they had little option if they wanted to remain at the inn, Casper was on close terms with the landlord and he only needed to say the word and they'd be kicked up their backsides, landing with a big thud on the cobbles outside, forced to live on the streets. 'You'll find Cassie downstairs, I've told her to keep something special for my two hard working lads.' He stood and patted Archie's head. Archie glanced at Smithy and could see the boy was well narked. Was he jealous as the old man was paying him a lot of attention or was it something else? Maybe Mr Casper realised the real state of play, that he, Archie Ledbetter, had managed to whip those items and Smithy hadn't done a stroke to get them but claimed all the credit.

When they left Casper's room and reached the courtyard below, Smithy said, 'The old git owes us far more than that! He'll get to keep most of it and will give the landlord a share and all. He also slips Cassie a little something for giving us grub and helping us out. He also slips her a little something else and all.'

'Something else?' Archie was puzzled.

'I'll tell you when you're older, Archie son.'

Archie wasn't daft and guessed it was something to do with Casper being sweet on Cassie.

When they got downstairs to the kitchen, they found a young maid at the sink washing the dishes who only looked a bit older than them. Her dark curly hair flowed from beneath her mobcap and she had dark shiny eyes and a freckled face, but Archie thought she was the most beautiful girl he'd ever set eyes on in his life. 'This, here, is Lucy!' said Smithy proudly. 'She's me girlfriend.'

Lucy smiled and batted her eyelids as if quite shy. 'Hello!' she said, as scrubbed away at a pot covered in soapy suds.

'Hello!' said Archie.

'Cassie's left some food in the oven for you. It's been in there for some time but it should be fine for you to eat if you don't leave it any longer.'

Smithy opened the oven door. 'Smells 'orright to me, don't know what it is though?'

'A nice bit of rabbit for you both with some veggies and gravy.'

Lucy stood down from the old wooden crate which she'd been using to reach the sink. She dried her hands on a towel, then brought out two tin plates with a dinner on each for both of them.

It smelled fine to Archie but looked a bit shrivelled. He didn't much like the idea of eating a rabbit though.

'Sorry, it's a bit dried up,' Lucy explained, 'we had a lot to feed tonight and they all ate a lot earlier. You pair were busy with the horses and the coaches for so long I thought you were never going to sit down to eat.'

And blooming thieving, Archie thought.

It was the ostlers who took most care with the horses and he realised that he and Smithy were really here under false pretences by now. They mucked in, but their real mission was to steal off rich folk not act as stable boys.

After scoffing down his food which really didn't taste as good as their earlier meal, he wondered what tomorrow might bring.

***

During his sleep, Archie was awakened by the sound of horses' hooves on the cobbles. In the half-light he noticed Smithy stirring, and then the lad was immediately on his feet. 'It's the mail coach,' he explained. 'I forgot it was due this morning. They'll be looking for fresh horses.'

Archie scrambled to his feet, wiping the sleep from his eyes. 'What do we have to do?'

'Just help the ostlers. They'll dismantle the horses, we need to feed, water and rest them until they're required next. The ostlers will sort out the fresh horses.'

Archie ran to the stable door in time to see the mail coach enter the archway. He was overawed with how impressive the coach looked. The two black horses pulling it looked weary as they puffed out clouds of steam and their coats were covered in a thick sheen of sweat. The coach, itself, was a smart black one with fancy gilt lettering which read: "York to London", its red wheels in stark contrast to its black bodywork. "Royal Mail", was written on the doors either side, and there was a royal coat of arms too. A thought ran through his mind, if this was a mail coach, then maybe they could deliver a letter to his uncle if only he could think of the address. All he knew was that the house was called, Huntingdon Hall, but he had no address for the place. But as he watched for a chance to say something, he was to be severely disappointed as all that happened was a rapid turn over of the horses and the chance for the postal workers to have a quick bite to eat and drink before they were on their way again, so they scurried inside the inn.

'When's the next coach due to pass through?' he asked Smithy.

'Not for a few days, that one passes through twice a week. We don't get many calling here as this is one of the smaller coaching houses in London. Why?'

Not wanting to give the real reason, Archie said, 'I just wondered that's all.'

'C'mon,' Smithy urged tugging on Archie's jacket, 'Let's see if Cassie's got anything for us for breakfast.'

He had to admit he was starving again. The ostlers seemed to be strong and fit and were given special privileges at the inn, but he and Smithy were hangers-on, there by the skin of their teeth by the look of it and the benevolence of both Mr Casper and the landlord, who he'd been informed by Smithy was named, Mr Harrington.

By the time they'd arrived by the back door of the kitchen, all hell had broken loose. Lucy was running around in a blind panic and Cassie looked as though she'd been crying as her eyes were puffy and red.

'What's up with yer pair?' Smithy asked.

'A gentleman was robbed of his wallet here last night,' Lucy explained. 'The police are on their way and we're being blamed.'

'But it was…' Archie was about to explain when Smithy grabbed hold of his arm roughly and kicked him on the back of his leg.

'Was what?' Lucy's eyes widened and she wrinkled her cute little button of a nose.

'It was shocking, weren't it, Archie?' Smithy said. 'Old Casper just told us.'

Archie nodded. 'Y…yes.'

'But why do people think it's one of you two?' Smithy asked.

'Because we were both in and out of the bar room at some point during the evening. According to the customer, who it appears is some fancy London lawyer, a lad bumped into him in the bar, but the landlord says no, there was no boy in the bar last night whatsoever, he'd have noticed. So now the customer thinks it's one of us!'

'Can't he remember then?' Archie asked.

Lucy shook her thick curls. 'No. All he remembers is some young person bumping into him and he gave them a clip around the earhole. He was blotto, I remember him slurring his words. Now people will think it's definitely me and not Cassie as I'm so young.'

Archie let out a long breath. This wasn't fair at all. He really felt for the girl but Smithy didn't seem that bothered considering she was his girlfriend.

After they'd eaten the buttered crumpets Cassie had put to one side for them and were back in the stable with Duke, where they'd brought him some left-over bacon scraps, Archie said, 'I think it's best if I own up. I don't want Lucy getting into any trouble because of me, and if the police have hold of me, then perhaps they can help me get back home to my uncle.'

Smithy laughed nervously. 'Now don't be too hasty, me old son…' He sat on the floor beside Archie and wrapped an arm around him. 'We're blood brothers now, ain't we?'

Archie nodded. 'Suppose so.'

'What good would it do to dob yerself in as if you do the rozzers will take you in for questioning and break you. Then they'll find out that Mr Casper, the landlord, and the rest of us, are in on this together and we'll all end up in prison on rations of bread and water!'

'I hadn't looked on it like that,' Archie said with his head lowered.

'There you go then. Say nothing for now.'

'But Lucy—'

'Lucy is a sweet an innocent gal. The police will realise that once they speak to her. Besides, she won't have any hot property or money on her person, will she?'

He supposed not, which made him feel a little better about the situation.

***

A detective and a uniformed constable arrived on the scene shortly afterwards. The detective had the bushiest sideburns Archie had ever seen and all the time he was there, he held a pipe in his hand, which he smoked intermittently. The uniformed constable was sent hither and thither to fetch people to be interviewed whilst the detective sat in a leather highbacked armchair in the coffee room of the inn. Archie thought he looked like he was enjoying all the palaver whilst his subordinate was so rushed off his feet, his cheeks were ruddied red and he was breathless in pursuit of particular people.

When it was Archie's turn to be questioned he stood with his hands behind his back.

'What's your name, son?' The detective puffed out a plume of acrid smoke that hit Archie's throat giving him the urge to cough, which he fought to suppress.

'Archie Ledbetter, sir.'

The detective nodded. 'And how long have you worked at this establishment?'

'I started here just yesterday, sir.'

The detective sat forward in his chair and narrowed his eyes. 'Most interesting indeed. And where were you after 10 o'clock last night?'

'Out in the yard, we were cleaning the coaches, sir. Then we had some grub and went to sleep in the stables.' He'd been coached by Smithy as to what to tell the detective.

'And you didn't see the gentleman who had his wallet stolen?'

Archie shook his head. 'No, sir, I did not.'

'Maybe,' said the detective, 'we could refresh your memory?'

Puzzled, Archie stood his ground but then felt his legs buckle beneath him as the detective carried on. 'Police Constable Samson!' he shouted through the open door.

Samson arrived within seconds, still looking red-faced though not as breathless. 'Sir?'

'Can you show Mr Fortescue into the room, please?'

A looming figure entered the coffee room, well dressed in a brocade waistcoat, long frock coat with black velvet trim and pinstriped trousers. He glared at Archie, his eyes seeming to bulge out of his head as his cheeks inflated, seemingly with fury.

'Is this the boy you smacked around the head, Mr Fortescue?' the detective asked.

Fortescue narrowed his gaze. 'I can't say for certain, but he's about the right height of what I remember. I was tired and I admit I'd partaken of a little too much gin.'

The constable whispered something in the detective's ear. 'Good idea, Samson…' he said. 'Bring in the girl and we can compare their heights, it has to be one or the other. All the other young folk who were present at this establishment have good alibis. That Smithy lad was seen by several people, including the coach driver, cleaning down the coach, though interestingly enough, none saw this young man stood before me!'

The detective's voice was now beginning to sound quite irritated to Archie and he badly needed to pee.

Oh no, I hope I don't cough right now as I'll wet myself!

The constable left the room leaving a long awkward silence in his wake, returning a couple of minutes later with Lucy by his side, who seemed all of a tremble, her big brown eyes looking so sad that Archie wanted to hug her and tell her all would be well, but he didn't know that for sure. Archie felt really sorry for the girl as she had done nothing wrong whatsoever and he was to blame.

The detective addressed her. 'Where were you, miss, from 10 o'clock onwards last night?'

She swallowed hard. 'I'd been helping the cook in the kitchen, serving the men grub, then I went to the bar room.'

'And what were you doing there?'

'I was helping to take drinks to some of the men and collecting their empties. I was a bit irritated to be 'onest with you, sir.'

'And why was that?'

'Because I was busy enough in the kitchen as it was, I had a stack of pots and pans that needed washing full of hardened on food, so they'd need some good ol' scrubbing an' all. I fought to meself, how can I be in two places at once? Well, it's just not possible is it?'

The detective nodded. 'Have you ever seen this gentleman before?' He pointed to Fortescue.

'Y…yes. He was in the bar last night and I also saw him check in earlier on that day.'

The detective turned his attention to the man. 'Did you see this girl in the bar room last night, Mr Fortescue?'

'I don't rightly remember. I don't take much notice of skivvy sorts…but she could be the right height of the person I walloped after they bumped into me.'

Archie watched as Lucy's cheeks flamed. The man had insulted her and he felt like walloping him himself.

There was another silence as if the detective was mulling things over. 'To be honest with you, I think there is a lack of evidence in this case.' He turned to Samson. 'Did the men check the boy's sleeping area and the girl's?'

The constable nodded. 'Yes, sir. Nothing was found.'

'Turn out your pockets, both of you!' the detective demanded and he narrowed his gaze as he glared at them.

Archie pulled out the pockets of his kegs and his jacket and the constable checked them. 'Nothing here, sir,' he declared. Archie was extremely thankful that he'd covered his tracks earlier, afraid this might happen.

The constable then checked Lucy's dress and apron pockets. 'Nothing here either, sir,' he said.

Whew, that was a close one, Archie had hidden his ill-gotten gains, including the money he got from a customer, beneath an old wooden floorboard in the stable area. He'd done it to keep it safe from Smithy really as now he just didn't trust the lad, but thank goodness he had.

The detective stood and looking Mr Fortescue square in the face said, 'From what I can see, you were very careless last night and drank too much spirit, sir. You should have had your wits about you in a place like this. People like you are prime targets for pilfering!'

'W...what?' The man seemed astounded that now the detective was turning on him.

'If you had remained sober last night, this would have been an unlikely occurrence. I suggest in future you stay off the gin and keep your valuables under lock and key. And I am far from impressed that you can't even tell the sex of the young person who bumped into you. Now, I could bring a case against you, for wasting police time!'

Fortescue looked outraged as his lips set in a thin line. 'And I, sir, have the powers to bring a case against *you*, as I am a top city lawyer.'

The detective just smiled at him as if he was quite mad. Then he turned to Lucy and Archie and said, 'You are both free to go.'

Archie let out a long breath of relief and followed Lucy out of the room. They'd had a lucky escape. He now knew he couldn't stay here for much longer, he had to get away soon.

Once outside in the corridor, much to his amazement, Lucy hugged him. 'I'm so pleased the police didn't catch you, Archie.'

He blinked several times. 'You knew?'

She nodded and then whispered, 'They bring in new lads here all the time to do that job and Smithy always takes advantage of them when Mr Casper asks him to help out on their first time. If you stay here much longer then you really will get caught by the police and you could end up transported to Australia.'

He gulped. He wouldn't want to go so far away, it was on the other side of the world, or so he'd been told. He'd never get to see his uncle, Cook and Polly again if he went there. Ginny wouldn't know where he was either. 'I was just thinking that myself. But where can I go, Lucy?'

At that point, Cassie passed by and glared at the pair of them. 'You young folk know nothing! Transportation to Australia ended a few years back!' She walked off in a huff as she headed towards the kitchen.

Lucy laughed. 'Don't pay any attention to her, I think her brother was sent there for nicking a leg of lamb from the butcher or something, she's never got over it!'

'I don't know if it's still going on but I don't want to end up there! I need to find a safe place to stay.'

Lucy's eyes shone brightly as if she'd just had an idea. 'I've got an auntie who might be able to sort you out, she runs a bakery a few streets over. As long as you're a willing worker, which I can see you are, she might take you on. Meet me first light in the morning, come to the kitchen door and I'll take you there.'

For the first time since staying here, Archie felt this was someone he could trust at the inn.

Chapter Eleven

Flora and Bobby had settled well into the house
where they'd been allocated a small attic room to
share. As a maid of all work Flora was expected to do
all manner of things, everything from raking out the
ashes of the coal fires in each room, to polishing the
furniture, to even serving the family who lived at the
house their meals. Although the work was arduous,
she didn't mind one bit because she didn't have the
fear around her any longer of being hit over the head
by a big brute or taken forcefully at any given
moment to satisfy his sinful urges. Bobby seemed
happy enough too, although he missed Duke and
Archie something rotten. When Flora was working
during the day, he either tried to give her a hand, or
stayed in their room reading a book he'd been given
by one of the maids or else he played with his
marbles on the floor. He soon got bored though as his
mother now worked long hours to keep them fed and
with a roof over their heads. From the attic window,
he'd noticed a small gate at the back of the garden
and had taken to sitting outside and reading instead
on nice days. He could barely read or write really, not
like Archie who was good at it, but nevertheless, he
enjoyed looking at the colourful pictures in some of
the books. He wondered what would happen if he just
sneaked out of the garden and went for a walk on his
own. Would anyone even miss him? His mother said
she wouldn't return to their room for a couple more
hours and the days were so long without her at his
side.

Standing on tiptoes, he clicked the latch and
pushed the gate open, finding himself standing in a

long lane which was flanked either side by some tall trees. The leaves were now turning the colours of burnished copper and vibrant red and as the breeze hit, they fluttered to the ground carpeting it like a great autumnal tablecloth. Now, which way should he go? Right or left? He thought for a moment? He had one green and one blue marble in his jacket pocket. If he picked the green one he'd turn left, if he picked the blue he'd go right.

He fumbled around in his pocket, then picked one and held it up to the light. It was the blue one. Right, it was then. He was about to set off on an adventure just like that man Robinson Crusoe that Archie had told him about!

***

Mrs Harper's bakery could be located a few streets away from the coaching inn. Archie had to sidestep several piles of horse manure and rubbish underfoot and the area stank to high heaven. At one point he was about to kick some old "rubbish" out of the way when the pile suddenly moved, groaned and got up and walked away. He realised it was a person lying there. It reminded him of the folk at Itchy Park a couple of nights ago. Couple of nights ago? It seemed like a lifetime had passed since then. He carried on following Lucy who was marching purposely towards her aunt's place, trying to keep up with her and realising she wanted to get back to the kitchen in time for her shift. It was still early and Duke seemed wary of the area, intermittently growling from time-to-time but at what in particular Archie had no idea.

He finally caught up with her. Breathlessly he asked, 'What's the rush? I know you have to get back to work, but you seem on pins?'

'It's not a good area at all this part,' she explained, her dark brown curls bouncing on her shoulders. 'Be very wary if you have to come here. They'll slit your throat as good as look at you for a few pennies!'

Oh dear, what was he letting himself in for? He might be less safe here than he was at the inn or with Bill Brackley going up chimneys!

Finally, they turned a corner and entered a much more civilised looking street. Lucy held firmly on to her basket. 'I'm going to pretend I was borrowing some suet from my aunt, in case I get asked any questions on my return,' she explained.

They stood outside the house which, although looking more run down than the one Flora and Bobby had been taken into, he could see at one time it had been a grand house indeed. Lucy made her way up the uneven steps and rapped the door. The blue paint was peeling off it but it looked a real solid looking door, much better than the one they'd lived behind in Dock Street.

Presently, it was opened by a middle-aged woman who, when she saw them there, wrapped her arms around her niece with tears in her eyes. Archie didn't get it. Why was she upset to see Lucy? The woman began to smile and chat with the girl and then looking over Lucy's shoulder at Archie, waved at him. Archie thought he'd better tie Duke's lead to the railings outside in case Lucy's aunt didn't like dogs, but he hoped she did. It was not a moment before all three were seated inside the house and talking to one another animatedly, Lucy having explained she had to return to the inn soon but would be back later.

When she'd departed, the lady who'd been introduced to him as Bessie Harper, said, 'So, yer after a job then, Archie?'

He nodded. 'Yes, ma'am.'

She bit her bottom lip. 'I can't think that I've got a lot for you at the moment as I've just taken a new boy on though he is a little lazy, needs a swift kick up the backside. I could do with someone to deliver the pies for me as to be truthful it's too much for one person to man the market stall and deliver as well. Could you do that? I have a wooden cart, you'd have to push it to the houses and pubs in the area.'

He nodded, keen to get started. Then his face fell when he thought of Duke outside. As if reading his mind, Bessie said, 'Go and untie your dog and bring him in, Archie, then you can both have something to eat!'

His face broke out into a big grin. 'Thanks, missus!'

'You can both sleep in the kitchen at night, there's a curtained off area at the back so you'll have some privacy and it's nice and warm there beside the stove, but be warned…' She held up her index finger as Archie waited with bated breath. 'You'll be woken up early by the kitchen staff clattering around!'

He nodded, he didn't mind that as he was more of a morning person than a night one. He hadn't much liked being up late last night at the coaching inn. His stomach lurched when he realised that Casper and Smithy would have missed him by now and he hoped that no one thought to question Lucy about his sudden disappearance.

***

After he'd filled his belly and Duke had been fed a few leftover scraps of pie crusts which he'd relished with delight, Bessie showed Archie to the wooden cart which was stowed away under a piece of tarpaulin in the backyard. It was a heavy looking thing that bore the name "Bessie Harper, Purveyor of Pies" on each side in thick red lettering outlined in gold.

'Now, you're to set off with that cart, lad, and are to deliver to several houses in the area. Can you read, Archie?' It was as if the thought had only just occurred to her.

He nodded, and beaming said, 'I can read very well, Mrs Harper!' He wondered though where the pies were, he'd only seen evidence of them in the crusts that the woman had fed Duke. There was no sign of any baking going on in the house.

As if realising his thoughts, she said, 'Come along with me…' She led him down the backyard past an area which had a flower bed on one side of the path and another dug up area on the other side, which he guessed might be for vegetables, going by the long bamboo sticks that were arranged near the wall. He'd seen Mr Featherstone doing the same thing back at the big house to grow runner beans and peas. Thinking of Mr Featherstone made him nostalgic for the place. He hadn't realised how well he'd settled in there until now when life had got so tough for him, but he reminded himself he was a darn sight better off than he'd been the day before being at the beck and call of an old thief and his accomplices, and even better off than the day before that when he could be forced up sooty old chimneys. So he had a lot to thank his lucky stars for.

Mrs Harper flicked the rusty iron latch on the back gate of her property and led him through to a small building on the opposite side of the back lane. It had a couple of steamy looking windows and a chimney, too, that puffed out clouds of steam. It looked like a house but was quite small in contrast to most houses. 'This is where I bake me pies!' She said proudly as she opened the door. It was quite hot inside and he noticed two young lads, a bit older than himself, who were dressed just in their white vests and trousers as it was so hot. One of the boys was pulling a tray of pies out of the oven, using a couple of thick cloths not to burn himself. My, they did smell good. Although he'd been fed, Archie felt his mouth watering at the thought of the thick flaky pastry, meat and gravy inside. The other lad was placing some pies in a big wicker tray on the counter.

'These are my sons, Jacob and Harry!' she announced as proudly as when she'd mentioned this was her bakery.

Jacob, who was the taller of two, had a scrappy ginger beard as if he'd only just started growing it. He scowled at Archie behind his mother's back, but Harry seemed friendly enough.

'Hello, mate!' he said, with a big grin on his freckled face.

'Hello,' said Archie to be polite.

'Archie's going to be working for me lads, taking on your round, Jacob.'

Jacob narrowed his eyes. 'But I get plenty of tips on that round!' he protested.

'It'll give you longer to sell at the market, and I think that way we'll make even more money!' His mother explained.

Jacob rolled his eyes. It was evident he wasn't at all happy at Archie's sudden arrival and he hoped he wouldn't make an enemy of the lad.

The round Mrs Harper had lined up for Archie was quite straightforward. She explained there were a few regular customers on the same streets and there were a couple of pubs he had to deliver to as well. He did worry though about bumping into Smithy or Casper being in that particular area, but Lucy had explained to him that the poor place they had passed through was the dividing line between the haves and have-nots in the area. There were a different class of people here altogether.

***

Bobby found himself at the end of the road, looking back at the house. He wouldn't be missed for a while yet, and to his delight, he noticed a small park ahead of him. It was nothing like that Itchy Park they'd dossed down in recently that his ma told him was an area of London known as "Spitalfields". That park didn't even have any swings or a lake, just gravestones and smelly bodies lying around everywhere. This park had a big seesaw, a couple of swings and a small pond. It also had lots of trees and pretty flowers. He could come here to read his books when his mother was busy at work and no one need ever know about his disappearance. He watched in envy as he saw a man and two children enter the park.

He must be their father, he thought to himself. How he'd love to have a proper father. The nearest he'd ever got to a father was Bill Brackley. But what sort of a father sent his son up a chimney and forced him to sleep on the floor under a pile of coal sacks!

The children looked well dressed. Shouldn't that man be in work today? Then he remembered it was the weekend. Maybe the man was so wealthy that he didn't have to work on a Saturday.

***

At the other end of the park lurked a figure in shabby dress, who had just noticed Bobby. He was in the area to pick up payment for his services as a chimney sweep, there were one or two customers who still owed him money and he intended to charge them extra for keeping him waiting and all.

He smiled to himself. *So, this is where the lad has ended up. But he's with a wealthy-looking gentleman and two children? Maybe he's the owner of one of the houses around these parts and he's taken Bobby with him out of pity. Perhaps he's employing the little scroat to keep his house clean along with that whore of a mother of his!*

But then it became evident that Bobby was with neither of them at the park as the boy ambled towards the gate, leaving the man and two children sailing a small wooden boat on the pond. Bill thought it in his best interests to follow after him.

***

People were friendly enough as Archie dropped of the pies in Nightingale Terrace. He even got a few coppers here and there from the cooks at the big houses, and one even gave him a thrupenny bit. Most of the houses looked pretty much the same but how he loved gazing into those windows with their frilly net curtains and their flower pots outside their doors. Down the steps to the basements he had to go to deliver mind, so he couldn't afford to stare too long. And down there he'd smell the most delicious aromas as meals were being prepared for those upstairs. Oh yes, it really was an upstairs/downstairs world in these parts. Where he'd come from he hadn't known such a world existed. The only person he'd thought of as posh was Queen Victoria herself. Now she lived in a right palace, but wasn't it too big for one person? Didn't make much sense to him, but his mother had explained to him how she had to have so many staff. Maids for this, that and the other were needed, footmen too, butlers, and all sorts. Cooks and cleaners, men to deal with the horses and even guards! Why should one lady need so much?

He came back to earth as he heard someone say gruffly. 'Come on, lad, we haven't got all day!' He'd come face-to-face with a smartly dressed, elderly man at the basement of one of the houses and by the look on his face, he wasn't best pleased with Archie neither. 'These pies should have been here half an hour since!'

'S...sorry, sir, it's my first day on the job.' Archie hadn't been expecting this, why hadn't Mrs Harper or one of the boys warned him? But then again, he realised he had been dawdling a bit as everything was so new to him.

'Never mind your excuses, place them on the table in there, please.'

Archie carried a small wicker tray of pies that had been marked up for the address into the kitchen and placed them on the pine table. There was no one else around.

For a moment, Archie feared he'd get a clip around his earhole because he was late, but then the man softened and said, 'I suppose I'm being a bit hard on you, son, as it's your first day and you've probably got a lot of places to go?'

Archie nodded, afraid to say anything for fear of getting into further trouble.

'It won't hurt them to have to wait a little longer upstairs.' He chuckled. 'I'm Henry Baxter, the butler here. Sit down for a moment, lad, in that chair while I give these to Cook.' He left Archie for a moment, who was unsure what to do. He really should get on with his work, but this man might be mad at him if he didn't stop here until he came back.

Presently, the man who was dressed in a long black jacket, matching trousers, a white shirt and black tie, returned. Archie also noticed he wore white gloves, just like Simpkins did at Huntington Hall.

'Now then, young fellow, I'm on my break for a few minutes, so I've asked Cook to send one of the maids to us with a teapot and two cups! Now if you're around this way at this time most days we can have a cuppa together!'

Archie's eyes enlargened. He hadn't been expecting this at all.

The maid, Tilly, arrived with a tray of tea and some scones. 'They're left over from yesterday, Mr Baxter,' she exclaimed. 'A bit stale but they should do.'

Baxter smiled and thanked her whilst Archie nodded his thanks. The pair of them got along famously as Archie explained who he was and all that had happened to him in such a short space of time.

'I really think we need to get you back to your uncle, Archie,' he said rubbing his chin thoughtfully. 'When I get a chance I shall speak to the master of the house. Maybe he's heard of Huntington Hall or can ask around.'

'Thank you, sir, that would be smashing!' Archie said, wiping the stray jam and cream from his mouth with the handkerchief Ginny had given him. He'd kept it all this time. Mrs Harper had even washed it for him so it was nice and clean.

And so for the next few days, Archie completed his pie round with pride and always made time to call to see Mr Baxter who had no family of his own and had come to regard the boy in a fatherly fashion.

***

Bill watched Bobby strolling down the lane with his hands dug deep in his pockets as he whistled a merry tune. Pity he didn't realise that his merry days were now numbered! The boy stopped at the back gate of one particular property and, standing on tiptoes to reach the catch on the top of the wooden gate, entered the back of a property. Oh, he recognised the house all right, it was the one where they'd swept the chimneys recently, but what was Bobby doing there? He frowned. But if the boy was there then his mother would be too. He was going to get the bitch back by hook or by crook. Now wasn't the time as it was broad daylight and there might be too many folks around.

She'd pay the price for leaving him, that she would.

After he'd collected payment on the same street, there was a coaching inn he needed to call into, what was it called now? The Horn and Bugle! That was it, someone had told him in the pub the other night they were looking for someone to sweep the chimney there. Well he was going to have to get Bobby back to do that, wasn't he? He'd call in there too afterwards to tell them he could sweep for them in a few days, meanwhile, he'd make out he had a lot of work on. He didn't in reality as he had no boy to work for him right now, but they didn't know that, did they? By then he'd have Bobby back and he'd work him harder than ever.

Without Flora around, he found himself unable to scratch his salacious itch. He'd heard about some floosie sorts who hung around that coaching inn, one worked in the kitchen if he was desperate. An older woman, not so great looking, called "Ginger" by all accounts, but who looked at the mantelpiece when they were poking the fire anyhow? She'd be cheap at half the price that would be for sure, in all sorts of ways, he chuckled to himself.

***

After picking up payment from some of the houses, where the housekeepers had protested that the price had gone up but paid up anyhow, Bill made for the coaching inn. When he arrived he went straight to the bar for a pint and spoke to the landlord, Mr Harrington, about the job in question. To his relief, the man was happy for him to start work in a few days' time. As he stood by the bar, he noticed an old man with a hooked nose wearing a wideawake hat enter, with a young lad at his side. He strained to listen to what they were saying.

'I'm telling you now, Mr Casper, it weren't my fault the boy escaped. I got up and he was gorn, cleared out, the dog an' all. After all we done for him!'

Bill had only been listening out of interest, having nothing better to do, but now his ears pricked up at the mention of a boy and a dog.

'Well next time we get a new lad, I'm putting you on watch, or I won't give you any payment if he goes missing. That lad was worth good money to us!'

The lad scowled and went to sit in the corner.

Bill's eyes met with those of Mr Casper. 'I'm sorry, sir,' he said, shifting closer and putting on a more refined voice than usual. 'I couldn't help overhearing that you had a dog and a lad here recently?'

The old man narrowed his eyes. 'What's it to you?'

'Aw,' said Bill. 'The lad was working as a chimney sweep and made off with all my takings!' It was a lie of course, but one employed to gain sympathy and it worked.

'Could be the same boy, I suppose,' said Casper. 'What did he look like? And the dog? Any descriptions?'

Bill nodded slowly. 'He's ten-years-old but small for his age. Dark hair, slight build. The dog is an Irish wolfhound, goes by the name of "Duke".'

The old man nodded eagerly. 'Those are the ones I was talking about, boy's name is "Archie". Maybe we could join forces to find them?'

Bill grinned. 'Let me pay for your pint, me fine fellow!' He slapped the man on the back, having no intention of helping him find the boy, but he'd get all the information he could glean out of him to satisfy his own ends.

Chapter Twelve

Moonlight streamed in through the small attic window. Bobby couldn't sleep, beside him his mother snored gently. She was worn out from all the work she did at the big house. She seemed to be constantly busy and had few breaks. She wasn't due a day off until the end of the month neither and that would have to be a Sunday. It was so lonely being on his own all of the time. An idea was beginning to form in his mind. Why not go to the park? There'd be nobody there this time of the night. He shouldn't be scared, should he? After all those dark chimneys he climbed up.

Quietly, he got out of his bed and changed from his nightshirt into his sensible day clothes and, closing the door behind him, made his way down the narrow winding stairs until he made the main landing. It was as if the whole household were asleep. He couldn't hear any noise at all here, apart from the ticking of the grandfather clock. He'd slip out and be back before anyone noticed he was missing.

He was careful to leave the back door of the house on its latch so he could slip back in later. Although the moon cast a beam of light illuminating his pathway, it was still eerie as the moon itself seemed large and full, and somewhere in the distance an owl hooted loudly. There was no clatter of cartwheels at this time of the morning, only the rustle of the wind blowing through the trees as he approached the park. Maybe he could have a little go on the swings and then head back to bed. He felt at peace in the park that was the only way to describe it.

Gingerly, he pushed open the park gate and made his way over to the swings. The light from a nearby gas lamp made it easy for him to see. He sat on the swing and pushed himself off the ground with his feet. High he went, higher and higher, all his cares drifting away. Faster, faster. Whoah, now he was really flying, but it wasn't himself making the swing fly high, someone was now pushing him. He felt the pressure of two strong arms forcing him up to the sky

Fear overtook him, it was too high for him to throw himself off the swing without hurting himself. The strong smell of alcohol enveloped his senses as he trembled all over, wetting himself in the process. Then he heard a familiar gruff voice say, 'Hello, Bobby! Yer little guttersnipe! You're coming home with me!'

***

When Archie arrived back at the bakery, Jacob glared at him. 'Took your time didn't you, rag o' muffin!'

Archie didn't want to tell him he'd spent time talking to Mr Baxter. 'I got a bit lost...' he lied.

Jacob narrowed his eyes. 'That's an easy round, you must be thick or something if you couldn't find your way around. Now wipe down those counters over there and sweep the floor! And if you get any tips in future you're to give them all to me! Understood?'

Archie nodded.

'Now turn out your pockets!'

Archie did as he was told as he feared the boy so much and was forced to hand over the thrupenny bit he'd been given earlier.

'You'll tip up to me every day or else yer'll feel the back of my hand!' Jacob growled, prodding him in the back. 'I could easily get you thrown out on to the streets so you'll end up in the workhouse! And don't forget it!'

Mrs Harper hadn't told him he had to do any of that cleaning Jacob mentioned, but while he did so, he noticed the lad was sitting down on an old wooden barrel watching his every movement, whilst he savoured an apple. Most of the debris was flour dust on the counter that needed brushing off and washing down, but some of the bits of leftover pastry adhered to it were sticky and messy to wipe clean. When he'd done that, all the while under the eagle eyes of Jacob, he picked up the hardwood brush the lad had handed him and began to sweep the floor.

'Don't forget those corners!' he growled.

When Archie'd finished what was asked of him, he let out a long breath of relief and was just about to return to the house to see Mrs Harper as she said she'd have something ready for him to eat, when Jacob got off the barrel and lifted Archie roughly from the floor by the collar of his jacket. 'Don't go thinking you're going to get an easy ride of it 'ere, mate! Far from it. Now before you leave, you can get that tray of pies out of the oven.' He looked behind him. Archie wished Harry was here right now as he was sure he wouldn't allow his brother to speak to him that way, but there was no sign of him and he wondered where the lad was.

As Archie gingerly opened the oven door, he stepped back as he felt the blowback from the heat.

'See that in there!' Jacob growled. 'You step on my toes and you'll end up in there, me darlin'! Burnt to a bleedin' crisp you'll be an' all! In fact, you might end up in one of me ma's meat pies!' He roared with laughter, throwing back his head maniacally as if he were possessed by something or other.

Archie stared at the fiery furnace within. Trembling, he felt the perspiration run down his neck, his mouth was dry and he longed to get out of the bakehouse. He heard a door open behind him and saw Harry stood there with an empty wicker basket cradled in his arms. 'More pies for the Palace Pub!' he announced, then seeing the look on Archie's face said, 'What's going on here?'

Jacob, who by now had ceased laughing, glared at Archie, daring him to say something.

'N...nothing,' Archie said. 'I need to get back to the house in case your ma needs me!'

He heard the echo of laughter as with lowered head he walked past Jacob and then Harry, into the alleyway outside. Placing both hands on his knees, he fought to catch his breath as he bent over. That was so scary back there, he feared Jacob more than he did Bill Brackley at the moment and that was saying something. Before going to sleep that night he knelt down and placing the palms of his hands together, uttered a little prayer:

Dear Lord God, please send your angels by morning to take me away from this place. Wherever I go I seem to meet wrong 'uns who want to hurt me and work me so hard that I can hardly stand or get me to do things I feel are wrong. I'm sorry for taking stuff that didn't belong to me at the inn, truly I am.

And by wrong 'uns I don't mean Mrs Harper of course as she has been kindness itself. Please if you could think of sending a couple of your angels, if they're not too busy that is, to take me from this earth to be with my Ma once again, I would be forever grateful. Amen.

Archie's shoulders wracked with grief as all the upset since his ma had first got ill came back full force to greet him as he broke down in tears. Ma was no longer here to protect him. Never again would she tuck him into bed at night, nor would she be able to wipe away his tears, not unless he was somehow able to join her again. Maybe it would be better to leave this world than live in it without her.

***

If Bobby thought life had been bad for him before, it was even worse now with no mother to protect him against Bill's bad moods. Bill had decided the lad was fit enough to climb chimneys once again and he wanted Archie back and all. That boy was an asset, better than Bobby really.

'Now, tell me ag'in, you little rascal, where did you last see the boy? What happened that night you all left here and where's Duke gorn?'

Bobby began to tremble with the fear of feeling the back of Bill's big hand in case he threw a stinging blow at him. 'D...Duke is with Archie. I last saw Archie when they took me and my ma on at that big house, they couldn't take another boy and a dog as well. So he went looking for somewhere else to go.'

'Hmmm,' Bill rubbed his stubbled chin. He hadn't washed or shaved in days because that bitch had caused all this trouble for him and he'd been brooding

187

on it. Flora was the one who reminded him to wash if he got too dirty and boiled his filthy ingrained clothing in a big saucepan, prodding it every so often with a big pair of wooden tongs.

If that old gent at the coaching inn was right, then he was hot on the trail of Archie Ledbetter. It hadn't gone cold as yet. So the lad must have walked around until being taken on there and he'd been told the dog had stayed as well. He reckoned that someone else at that inn must know where Archie was and he intended finding out who that person was. He knew it wasn't the old fella, he was genuine about not knowing, he could tell. He wanted the lad back for his own ill-gotten gains.

Fat tears welled up in Bobby's eyes, threatening to spill down his cheeks.

'What's the matter with you, lad?' Bill scowled. 'You want to man up. I'm taking you to the pub later, we'll chuck a couple of gins down yer neck, that'll put hairs on your chest!'

Inwardly Bobby groaned, it was the last thing he needed, especially if he was needed to go up chimneys again the following day.

Bill puzzled over that coaching inn. He was going to go back there later to suss the place out. Find out a bit more, like. There was something else going on and the person behind it all would lead him to the pot of gold lying in wait for him at the end of the rainbow.

Later, as Bobby cowered in the corner of the inn, Bill placed a glass of gin in front of the lad. 'Here, sup this by the time I come back,' he growled. 'Now remember what I told you, keep your eyes and ears open. If anyone mentions Archie or the dog, lemme know. Got it?' He tapped the side of his own nose as if to indicate it was all confidential.

Bobby managed a weak smile. Where Bill was off to he hadn't a clue, but then he saw him tapping the backside of a middle-aged barmaid who was bending over clearing a table of discarded tankards and dirty plates, she turned and giggled. The landlord, who was behind the bar, nodded at Bill as if they had some sort of secret understanding with one another. Bobby watched as Bill threw some sort of coinage onto the bar top in front of the landlord, then he turned, put his arm around the barmaid and escorted her away.

Where were they going to and what on earth for? It seemed to Bobby as if Bill didn't even know the woman. So why was he being so friendly with her? He remembered to take a sip of his gin and just as he did so another young woman, who looked younger than the other barmaid, swept into the room and met his gaze. She was so pretty with dark brown eyes the colour of chocolate. Not quite as pretty as his ma though but she had a very kind face nevertheless.

He gulped as she approached his table. 'What are you doing on your own, young 'un?' she asked, with one hand on her hip, the other with a round metal tray held firmly to her body so that it was tucked under her arm.

'I'm waiting for Mr Brackley to come back...' he said meekly.

Her expression changed to one of understanding as she said, 'Oh, so he's the gentleman just gone with Ginger to her room?'

'I don't know what her name was but she was collecting glasses in here not long since,' he replied.

She nodded. 'Aye, that's her. They'll be gone a while yet, if I know that one!' She chuckled. Then her face took on a more serious expression. 'What are you drinking there?' She narrowed her eyes.

'Gin. Bill bought it for me and told me to sup it by the time he returns.'

She shook her head. 'And I'm betting you'd much rather a lemonade or ginger beer, right?'

He nodded enthusiastically. Much to his horror, she swept the glass away with her free hand. Oh dear, he'd get in trouble with Bill now, but then she smiled.

'Don't worry, little 'un, I'm only going to swap it for lemonade for you. I'll pour the gin back into the bottle that way Mr Harrington won't mind as he can sell it twice over!'

For the first time that day, he smiled. Not a put-on smile like he'd done for Bill, but a big beaming one. True to her word, the barmaid returned with a cold glass of lemonade for him. 'I'm Lucy,' she introduced herself. 'What's your name? I can't keep calling you "little 'un", can I?'

After taking a long swig of the sweet cool drink, he set down his glass, wiped his mouth on the back of his sleeve and said, 'Bobby. My name is Bobby.'

'That's all?' she frowned. 'What's yer last name?'

He shrugged his shoulders. 'I don't rightly know, miss.'

'Well, your last name, your surname should be the same as your father's.'

'Don't have no father.'

'Oh. I see, well never mind. At least I know your first name is Bobby now and you know my name an' all.'

He could see he was going to like Lucy, but a dreadful thought occurred to him—Bill had told him to keep his eyes and ears open. Now he was going to have to tell him the barmaid's name. If he did that, Bill would be much nicer to him yet, looking at how lovely and kind Lucy was, he didn't want to betray her.

'I have to get back to work now,' she whispered as Bobby noticed the landlord glance over in her direction.

He nodded, sad to see her go. It was to be another hour before Bill returned with a big grin on his face, reeking of some sort of strong flowery scent he'd smelled on the barmaid earlier. And all the while, he'd been away he'd felt so uncomfortable being in a room with a few men, some who looked very dubious indeed. But Bill must have asked the landlord to look out for him as when one fella had approached him and asked if he needed a roof for the night, the man had warned him off and sent him packing from the inn. In truth, he felt safer when Bill was around than when he wasn't and that was saying something. Bill slapped Bobby hard on the back. 'Glad to see yer've drunk yer gin!'

As he walked home with Bill he wondered about his mother. Would she think he'd run away? He daren't mention her name to him though for fear it made him angry, but he could tell he missed her company and as young as he was, he realised that in some way Bill had gone to Ginger for some form of comfort tonight.

***

Archie made sure to keep himself well out of Jacob's reach and he only entered the bakery when he had to. Luckily, since the nasty incident where he feared the lad would seriously burn him, he hadn't encountered him alone. Either Harry had been around or Mrs Harper, which was such a relief. So Jacob wouldn't have dared try anything on.

One morning when he was having a break chatting with Mr Baxter, the man's eyes suddenly took on an excited looking gleam. 'Archie, I've been waiting for this moment to tell you something, lad!' he said when all the other servants had left the kitchen. Archie sat forward in his seat. 'Remember how I said I'd ask the master to question around if anyone had heard of Huntington Hall?'

'Yes?' Archie's heart scudded a beat.

'Well, the master knows this businessman, Mr Proudley, who has heard the name. Is your uncle's name, Walter Brooking, by any chance?'

'Yes, that's him!' Archie jumped out of his chair. He was going home at last.

'I thought that was the name you'd told me but wasn't sure so needed to check. Don't be too hasty lad, be seated,' Mr Baxter commanded as Archie's face fell. 'What I was about to say was once it's confirmed, the master will send word to your uncle and he can collect you here. It may take a day or two. Explain the situation to Mrs Harper.'

'I will, oh thank you, Mr Baxter!' He felt like hugging the old man but knew that wouldn't seem appropriate. 'And please thank your master for me and Mr Proudley, too.'

'You'll have the chance to thank them yourselves as they both plan to be here when your uncle arrives. It's just we didn't know for sure it would be the same Huntingdon Hall, there might have been another.'

Archie felt like whooping for joy, just wait until he told Mrs Harper and Lucy, too. Duke would have a new home and he could even ask his uncle about taking Flora and Bobby with him. He bet his uncle could do with some more staff at that big house of his. He felt so happy, he could shout it all from the rooftops.

How he managed to complete the rest of his pie round, he had no idea as his mind went into overdrive, creating all sorts of possibilities.

He arrived back at Mrs Harper's house crashing into the back kitchen with such a clatter, the woman ran to see what was wrong.

'It's all right, Mrs Harper, I've just had some good news!' After telling the woman all about it, he finally said, 'I must tell Lucy. I'll nip over to the coaching inn.'

Mrs Harper was aghast. 'No, Archie,' she said firmly. 'I'll get Harry to nip over with a message for her to call here later, it's not safe for you to go there and you could get Lucy into trouble with her employer.'

He nodded. He wanted to thank Lucy for her kindness and he couldn't bear the thought of leaving here without saying goodbye. At least in a day or two he'd be well away from all the troubling influences in London and he'd be glad to see the back of bullying Jacob once and for all.

Chapter Thirteen

Bill had wheedled it out of Bobby that the young, helpful barmaid at the inn was called Lucy. If she'd been kind to Bobby then maybe she'd have helped Archie get away. He was going to call in and keep a watchful eye. It was a long time before he saw her put in an appearance and even then, he only realised it was her as the landlady called her by name. She was dressed as if about to go outside in her bonnet and shawl and over the crook of her arm she carried a wicker basket.

'I'll get you those pies then from my auntie's place!' She called across the bar room to the landlord, but there was something about her manner that made Bill realise she was up to something. Being quite wily himself and over the years dealing with all manner of people, he could usually tell when someone was being a bit shifty. He made to follow after her as she walked down the street, her luxurious dark chestnut curls bouncing on her shoulders. Aye, she'd be an asset to have around an' all. If he could procure her services he could make a mint. But for time being, unwittingly, she was a lure for Archie Ledbetter. He could guess the lad would be sweet on a girl like Lucy and, being the young gentleman he was, he wouldn't want to see her getting hurt neither!

He watched from a distance as she rounded the street corner and then he hurried after her. She passed through a very pitiful area that even he didn't frequent as it smelled to high heaven of death and decay. Who knew what you'd catch even setting foot in that place, but go after her he must!

Then she passed through an alleyway and as he followed her, he realised it was more of a nobs area, not like the streets he'd just followed her from. So this is where her aunt lived. He blew out a low whistle, maybe the old bird had a bob or two.

He watched as she walked up some steps to a three-storey house and rapped on the door. No servants entrance for that girl, which told him she was in well with that aunt of hers. Then he watched as the door opened and the girl swept inside. Now the question was, if young Archie was in there? He'd have to bide his time to find that out. He didn't have long to wait as he walked his way to the back entrance of the house up the back alley and noticed the bakehouse door opposite it was open. A young lad with copper red hair emerged through the door as if he needed a breather. The girl had mentioned taking pies to the inn, so no doubt the bakehouse was part of the premises, he reckoned.

The red-haired lad looked at him curiously. He had one of those scrappy, goat-like beards as if he'd only just recently started sprouting hair as he was turning into a man.

'Want some baccy to chew?' Bill offered.

The lad nodded as Bill handed him the paper wrapped package. 'Thanks, mister. I'm afraid the bakehouse will be closing soon, did you want anything?' The lad's voice was croaky as if it was breaking, he was definitely becoming a man by the look of things.

Bill shook his head. 'I'm after some information about a young boy you might know.'

The lad, who had vivid blue eyes, met Bill's with interest. 'Oh yes?'

'The lad's name is Archie Ledbetter, he's about so high…' Bill indicated Archie's height with his hand. 'He's got a dog called Duke with him. Do you know of the lad?'

'I might, I might not, mister.' He angled his head in a curious fashion as if weighing things up.

This was a smart lad in front of him, he knew not to give any information away until he was offered something else of value to him.

Bill dipped into his pocket and held up a half-crown coin. 'Now, I'll ask you again if you know the boy?'

The lad nodded and Bill dropped the coin into his outstretched, flour-dusted hand, which he snatched with relish. 'He's staying at our house, there!' he pointed, obviously having no qualms whatsoever about giving Archie's location away. 'He's in the house now with my cousin, Lucy, and me ma, Mrs Harper!'

Bill grinned then walked away. His hunch had been correct. The boy was useful to know and he didn't care much for Archie neither, that much was evident. His plan was going perfectly.

***

Archie was so pleased to see Lucy once again. The girl's eyes glittered with amber flecks of gold as he told her his news. Mrs Harper had prepared a special tea for them both of miniature cucumber sandwiches, fondant fancies and long glasses of cool lemonade.

'Don't worry though, Lucy,' Archie said, 'I'll write to you so we can keep in touch and maybe you can visit the big house someday.'

'That would be lovely!' she sighed. 'I've never been inside one of those big country houses before. But don't send any letters to the inn, not for Mr Casper or Smithy to see them. Send them to my auntie's house instead, that way I'll be sure to get them.'

He nodded. 'I will, no fear.'

'Now then, Archie,' Mrs Harper said finally, 'it's getting dark so we better leave Lucy get back to the inn.'

'I'll walk you,' Archie offered.

Lucy frowned. 'What if Mr Casper sees you?'

'Well I can at least walk you part of the way,' he enthused.

She looked at her aunt who nodded in agreement. 'Come straight back then, Archie!' she called after the pair. 'Take Duke with you.'

Archie returned to the table where Duke was settled beneath. In his haste to be alone with Lucy, he'd almost forgotten his loyal friend.

'Come along, Duke!' he called. Duke lifted his head and whined as if he couldn't be bothered to make the effort.

'I don't know what's the matter with that dog today,' Mrs Harper tutted, 'he's not been himself at all. Maybe you better leave him behind in case he's sickening for something...'

Archie had only ever seen the dog act like that once before and that was when Bill Brackley was in the vicinity. But Bill was nowhere around so he reckoned the dog must be ill like Mrs Harper thought.

***

Bill watched the pair head off towards the coaching inn, an evil sneer swept across his face. He was going to teach that boy a lesson for running out on him. By damn he would!

He kept his distance as he observed the couple walk through the archway that led them to the dangerous area known as *No Man's Land*. His reflexes cut in and he almost gagged from the smell of something rotten permeating his nostrils. It was like a mixture of rotting cabbage and mouldering flesh. That sickly sweet pungent aroma reminded him of a dead rat he'd once found beneath the floorboards at his old digs at the docks. There was no mistaking it. But in this area it might not have been a rat, a cat nor even a dog. It could be human flesh. Some people were scared to pass this way as many were never seen again, or so people had told him at the inn. Even the police feared setting foot here. It was all a bit of an abyss really.

He watched as Archie stopped and said something to the girl. Then to Bill's astonishment, he leaned over and planted a kiss on her cheek. Well, what did you know? That pair *were* sweet on one another as he'd suspected and he planned using it to his advantage, by heck he would.

***

Archie left Lucy and turned to head back to Mrs Harper's house. He whistled a happy tune as he went with hands dug deep in his pockets. He couldn't believe his good fortune that soon he'd be back home and Lucy would keep in touch. He realised that she was Smithy's girl really but the lad didn't know how to treat her properly. Oh yes, he planned on asking his uncle to intervene and offer her a job at his house. Perhaps as a kitchen maid? And he mustn't forget about Bobby and Flora neither.

He was so absorbed in his thoughts that he failed to hear the echoing footsteps behind him that were gaining on his own.

Quite suddenly a dirty, big hand clamped over his mouth as he struggled to breathe. And then he glimpsed the glare of steel.

A knife!

'Keep still or I'll slit yer gizzard!' The voice growled. It was a voice he recognised all right–Bill Brackley! There was no mistaking the rancid breath or body odour emanating from the man, it was him all right. All mixed together with the fumes of alcohol.

He swallowed hard and his heart almost stopped beating as the sharp edge of the knife rested against his Adam's apple, ready to slice it like Cook would slice an apple for one of her pies. He froze with fear. One false move and it could all be over. Forever.

'Now then, young Archie,' Bill carried on. 'I'm going to remove me hand from yer mouth and walk you back to the digs. Understood?'

Archie nodded, all the while well aware of the sharp steel blade near his throat.

'Now, I'll have this knife near your back as we walk, so no funny business or it goes straight inside you like a bayonet.'

Archie relaxed a little, it was evident that Bill wanted him very much alive. Then releasing a breath he said, 'B…but Mrs Harper—'

'Blow Mrs Harper! You're of use to me now. And I plan getting that pretty little girlfriend of yours to join forces with me little gang and all! She'd fetch a pretty price if I tout her around the place!'

Archie had no idea what Bill meant by that, but he knew the man was up to no good, but for time being he'd have to play along until there was chance of another escape.

***

'Mrs Stockley! Mrs Stockley!' Polly was in such a tizzy and out of breath when she approached the kitchen.

Cook was in the middle of stirring the beef stew, when she removed the large wooden spoon, set it down and placed a lid on the saucepan to simmer. Turning, she looked at Polly in amazement. 'What's the matter with you, girl?'

'I've just been told by the master that Archie's been found!'

'Never to goodness!' A big smile broke out on Cook's face. 'Where and how'd that come about?'

'A gentleman from Nightingale Terrace was asked by his butler if he'd heard of this house. He hadn't himself but he asked one of his friends, who fortunately had. Apparently, Archie had been a regular visitor to that house.'

Cook clucked her teeth and positioned the palms of her hands together as if in silent contemplation as she looked up at the ceiling and said, 'My prayers have been answered at last!' Then she turned to Polly

'But I don't see how Archie would be visiting some gentleman's house, those are posh houses in that place.'

'I don't understand it meself and the master hasn't explained how, but he's on his way there right now. The gentleman of the house is arranging a meeting.'

This was the best news Cook had heard in ages and she felt like dancing a merry jig in amongst the kitchen furniture. In fact she felt like leaping on the old table but she knew her old bones wouldn't allow her to do that, so instead she said, 'Polly get out the fondant fancies, let's celebrate with a nice cup of char!'

Polly nodded eagerly. 'Shall I fetch Mr Featherstone?'

'Yes, do that, he'll want to know but don't bother with Poker Face Linley. Can't stand to have her in my kitchen with that nose of hers stuck in the air, she'll bring down the conversation and create a bad atmosphere!'

Polly giggled, evidently understanding full well what Cook meant.

Oh, it was a merry afternoon and all as they chatted about Archie and how they couldn't wait to see him again. Cook planned on baking him one of her special apple pies, Polly said she'd get his bedroom ready for him and Mr Featherstone said he'd tell him he could help in the gardens any time. But they were all to be sorely disappointed. When the master returned that evening he was all alone. His face downcast and it appeared to Cook as if he was about to cry.

'What's the matter?' she asked. 'Where's Archie?'

'I'm afraid I have some bad news…' he stroked his chin, then addressing her, Polly and Mr Featherstone said, 'I turned up at the house in Nightingale Terrace as arranged, but Archie wasn't there. The butler told me he'd been working for a Mrs Harper, delivering pies to customers. Naturally, I sought her out and she explained that Archie, the previous evening, had wanted to say farewell to her niece as she'd helped him and taken him to her aunt's house so he could stop and have a job with her. The night he walked her to the coaching inn where Mrs Harper's niece worked as a maid, he failed to return home. He even left behind a dog he'd been taking care of…'

'A dog?' Mrs Stockley scratched her head. 'He didn't have no dog when he lived here, where's he come from?'

'I don't rightly know,' Walter carried on, 'but I've brought the dog with me, his name is Duke, apparently. Simpkins is feeding him right now and will bed him down for the night.'

'Any idea how Archie ended up at that pie shop, Mr Brooking?' Polly wanted to know.

He shook his head. 'It's all a bit of a mystery how he escaped the clutches of that Bill Brackley and ended up elsewhere. Now I fear we might never find him again. We were so near and yet so far…'

'But you're forgetting something important here,' said Polly. The master quirked an interested eyebrow. 'You've got the dog! If he and Archie were that close he might help lead you to him, or failing that, Archie will try his best to get home for his new found friend if that baker woman gets to tell him you now have the dog.'

The master nodded and smiled.

Now there was a thought worth hanging on to.

***

'Get in there, you young upstart!' Archie felt Bill's boot up his backside as he came hurtling in through the door of the old digs and landed heavily with a thud, after him seeming to fly through the air. He looked up from the floor to see Bobby stood over him, and pulling himself up onto his haunches, then rubbing his sore backside, stared in amazement at the boy.

'If I so much as find either of you trying to get out of 'ere, neither of you will be a pretty sight by the time I've finished with you!' he growled, causing both boys to tremble. Then he was gone and Archie heard a key in the door. They were being locked in.

'It's no use,' Bobby said settling down beside Archie on the filthy floor; it was evident the rooms now lacked a woman's touch. 'He'll kill us if we escape this time.'

'But we have to,' said Archie, 'as if we don't bad things will happen anyhow. How'd he get hold of you?'

'He found me by accident. I done a daft thing. When Ma was busy working at the house I'd get so bored so I'd slip off to a park just down the road on me own. He must have been watching me for days, I reckon, then took his chance. Now he knows where Ma is. So I think she'll be next.' As if just realising he was missing, Bobby asked, 'What happened to Duke, did he run away?'

'No,' Archie breathed out a sigh of relief. Thank goodness the dog hadn't wanted to go with him when Bill nabbed him in the street. He must have had a bad tummy after eating too many pie crusts. But then again, if Duke had been with him, would he have defended him? 'I left him under the table at Mrs Harper's house, he didn't want to go out that night. Think he might have eaten something that disagreed with him. He'll be safe with her. Thinking about it he was acting most oddly beforehand, maybe he realised Bill was around. At least Duke will be well cared for by Mrs Harper.'

Bobby smiled as if relieved the dog was safe. 'Who's Mrs Harper?' he blinked. Archie could tell the lad had been crying as his eyes looked red and puffed up.

'She was a kind woman who took me and Duke in, gave us shelter and in return I delivered pies for her. She was ever so nice. But before that, the day I left you and your ma at the big house, I met a young boy called, Smithy. He's a bit older than us. He reckoned he could get me a job with him at the coaching inn. At first, I thought it was going to be an honest job but after a while I realised I was expected to thieve from customers at the place. There were some right nobs there, a bit like my uncle. There was a gang of them at that coaching inn who were all in on it. A man called Mr Casper was behind it all. His room was full of stolen stuff, you should have seen it, Bobby. There were all sorts of fancy treasures!' Bobby's eyes widened.

'So you didn't like it at the coaching inn?'

'It was all right, I suppose, but I wanted to get away. There was a lovely girl working there called, Lucy. She was a maid. It was her what put me in touch with Mrs Harper, who was her auntie.'

Bobby nodded then brightened up. 'I know her! I met her the other night when Bill took me there!' He said with a note of excitement to his voice. 'She was very kind as when Bill went off with a barmaid for an hour she swapped me gin for lemonade!'

'Ah, that sounds like Lucy, she's ever so kind.' Something had just occurred to Archie, if Bill was drinking at the coaching inn did he have some idea he'd been staying there? It all seemed like too much of a coincidence to him.

Suddenly Archie felt so tired as if all the wind had been knocked out of his sails. 'There's something else, too,' he said drowsily. 'I would have been going home tomorrow as someone had helped find my uncle and delivered a message there. I was so looking forward to going home and all.'

Bobby patted his shoulder. 'Never mind, Archie. At least you know your uncle has some sort of idea where you are. Me ma doesn't about me.'

There was truth in Bobby's words and he really felt for the boy and, as his ma was no longer around, he was going to have to look out for him.

'I'm bloomin' starvin'' Archie said, as his stomach growled.

'It will get worse,' Bobby explained. 'I haven't eaten anything for a couple of days 'cos Bill's starving me to go up chimneys again. There's some water in a tin mug on the table.'

Archie nodded, then stood to take a sip and offered it to Bobby who shook his head. 'Come on sup up, mate. You have to keep your strength up if we're to get out of here.'

Bobby did as he was told and closed his eyes, resting his head against the table leg. He looked so weak that it worried Archie. Seemed he had come along at the right time to keep the lad going and to help him escape. How silly was he that he wanted Smithy to be his brother as he was overtaken by the lad's wit and charm when it was Bobby who was most like a brother to him.

Chapter Fourteen

The banging was getting louder. Cook clucked her teeth and lifted the lace curtain to peer out of the kitchen window. What was going on here? Mr Featherstone was bending over with a hammer in his hand, he appeared to be hammering nails into a large piece of wood. She rushed out of the kitchen and outside.

When he saw her, he turned all red-faced and flustered. 'I've had orders from the master to build a kennel for that dog called Duke,' he explained. Then she noticed a large wire-haired dog circling around the man, wagging his tail.

'So, this is Duke! He looks like an Irish wolfhound to me!' she exclaimed with great excitement in her voice.

'Aye, I reckon so. Long legged thing he is an' all!'

Relief flooded through Cook, she'd been worried something was up and maybe Bill Brackley had turned up trying to hammer in the door for that payment he claimed was still owing to him.

The dog came lumbering over and jumped up on Cook robbing her of her breath as he licked away at her cheeks.

'He seems to like you,' Mr Featherstone grinned and he pushed back the brim of his hat with his hand to get a better view.

'Oh go on with you,' she laughed. 'He can probably smell food on me, that's all. I've got a corned beef pie in the oven. Blooming heck, he's a big 'un an' all.'

Mr Featherstone stood upright and in a serious tone said, 'No, animals are like that, they can sense whether people are nice or not.'

'That's a good thing you're doing there, Mr Featherstone,' she beamed. 'Come inside when you're finished and I'll brew up. I've got a couple of leftover scones that I'll be bound you wouldn't mind eating up!'

He smiled back at her with a twinkle in his rheumy blue eyes and she blushed like a school girl. She'd always liked Mr Featherstone but it had only been lately that they'd got a little closer. He'd lost his wife to consumption last year and it only seemed now since her death that he was no longer keeping himself to himself. He seemed like a different man despite them both having worked at the estate since Walter was a baby. She remembered all the grand parties the Brookings had thrown over the years. People came from miles in their fancy carriages and they'd swept in through the front door as Simpkins welcomed them and maids took their fur capes and coats. The women would wear special dresses for the balls held here; there was a summer ball and always a Christmas one. No doubt they'd have their own dress designer to hand to make the latest model for them as they wanted to outdo all the other ladies by becoming belle of the ball! Their hair would be styled especially for the occasion too, swept up onto their heads and well secured with pins and adorned with ribbons or feathers. My, my, they were such lovely times. As Cook reminisced as she put the kettle on to boil on the hob, she longed for the old days when there was plenty of life in the house before Archie's mother had been ravished by a friend of the family. In Cook's mind, there was a before and an after and the after seemed to be a long period of mourning from which Walter Brooking had never quite emerged. She often wondered if he blamed his sister for the deaths of their parents. Broken hearted the both of them had been. Mrs Brooking, in the end, hardly left her bedroom. And Mr Brooking looked like a shadow of his former self. Being the kind folk as they were, when the twins were born, they were prepared to pay for their upkeep but the plan was to give them away to a childless couple they knew who'd bring both boys up as their own. Though that was never to be as Alicia, after her young baby died in her arms, on a whim, fled with Archie. She wasn't going to lose that one and all. Ironically, she took the lad into a very tough life where he was left alone anyhow when she suddenly passed away. Cook had been so sad to hear that from Mr Walter. The man trusted her as she'd been with the family for such a long time.

Sighing to herself, she heard the back door open and turned to see Mr Featherstone standing there with his cap in his hand. 'I think Margaret, it's time you started called me Albert,' he said with a big smile on his face.

***

It was a long time before Bill returned home. The first thing Archie knew was when the door opened wide and slammed loudly against the wall as he came crashing into the room. The smell of alcohol turned Archie's stomach as now he associated it with the man. He'd learned to keep quiet and pretend to be asleep because if he showed he was awake then he might suffer at Bill's hands. He was drunk, that much was evident, and he wasn't alone either.

There was someone with him.

As Archie covered himself and Bobby with some old coal sacks, he heard Bill draw out a chair, dragging it across the flagstone floor. 'Sit down, Casper!' he invited.

Mr Casper? What's he doing here?

'Thanks, Bill.'

As both men were sat around the table, Archie squinted to see what was going on. Bill was pouring them both a tot of rum from the bottle he'd noticed earlier on the table when he went to get the cup of water.

'Now then, I think I can put a bit of business your way,' Bill was saying.

'Oh, yes?'

'That young barmaid working at the inn...'

'Rosie, the eighteen-year-old?'

'No, not that one, the young gal, looks about eleven or twelve?'

'Lucy?'

'Aye, that's the one! Pretty young thing, dark hair and curls.'

'What would you want with her?' Casper sounded a bit uneasy.

Archie's heart started to thud, he knew he wasn't going to like this one little bit.

'She's just the right age, I can get plenty of work out of her...'

'What do you mean? She's already got a job as a maid. Do you intend to have her working for you here, Bill?'

'In a manner of speaking, my good fellow!' Bill had deliberately put on a posh accent there.

'And I don't expect it's just to clean up this place for you?' Casper said, with some concern in his voice. Maybe the man wasn't as bad as Archie had previously imagined.

Bill lowered his voice. 'There'll be a pretty penny in it for you if you can kidnap her from the inn.'

'I don't like the sound of it, Bill. I know what you're up to. You want to earn money from that young girl by making her work immorally for you, she's only a child!'

'But think how much we could make from her. We could auction her virginity to begin with. The nobs like that sort of thing as they know they won't get poxed up to high heaven. Then after that, we can do it again and again, there are ways to fool people into thinking the girl is still a virgin.'

'I don't like the sound of it at all!' Casper took his drunk and gulped, then slammed it down on the table. 'Thank you for the rum, Bill. But I'd rather not speak of this again and neither should you. I'll play no part in this, the girl is just a child. You'll end up in prison and goodness knows what would happen to that girl if you bring her here.'

There was the sound of Casper's chair dragging across the flagstones as he stood to leave.

'Well if you reconsider, I promise I'll pay you quite handsomely for your time to lure the girl here, otherwise I shall have to take her by force.'

'I shall have nothing to do with this!' Casper said quite sharply. 'And neither should you if you have a shred of decency about you!' There was the sound of retreating footsteps and of him slamming the door behind himself, and then Bill chuckling which sent a shiver down Archie's spine.

What was a virgin? He hadn't a clue.

'I knew you'd chicken out, old Casper me mate! Well, the sooner I get that young chick under me wing the better.' Bill's voice had more than a hint of menace about it which chilled Archie to the bone.

Then before he knew it, Bill was lumbering across the room and fell down heavily on his bed and quite soon he was fast asleep as he heard him snoring loudly.

Stealthfully, Archie rose and went to the door. He tried to open it but it was budged fast. He'd been hoping that maybe Casper hadn't closed it properly behind him, but where was the key? If he could find that then maybe he and Bobby could escape before the lad was too weak to walk.

**

The following morning Archie and Bobby awoke early, their stomachs growling with hunger. Bill was still fast asleep. Every so often he'd let out a grunt, a snuffle and a snore, then he'd go quiet and it would all begin again. At least while he was asleep they were safe as were Flora and Lucy, but if they didn't escape soon, they'd die of starvation, never mind anything else. Archie scrambled around in one of the cupboards to see what he could find, but there was no food to speak of, even the rats and mice would have to starve today. No doubt, Bill was getting well fed elsewhere like at the coaching inn or downstairs in the pub.

The pub downstairs!

Why hadn't he thought of it before, the landlady often pegged out washing in the yard in the morning or one of the barmaids did it for her, he'd wait until he saw her next and would attract her attention. He remembered the little book that Flora had kept to write her stories in- that would be useful, then he recalled with a sinking heart that he'd returned it to her the night they'd escaped. But then a vision of how she'd torn out a couple of pages so he could draw came to mind, but he hadn't got around to it as Bill had returned home before he got the chance. He found the pages still folded under his old coal sack. Now all he needed was a pencil or even a fountain pen, where could he find one of those? All he could find was a stub of a candle and some soot and ashes in the fireplace, those would have to do. He picked up the candle and rubbed it in the sooty mess, then wrote HELP on one sheet of the paper in big letters, it was a good job he could write because he knew Bobby couldn't. It saddened Archie that Flora'd felt it necessary to hide that book from Bill. It was as if the brute didn't want Flora to have a life of her own.

Archie noticed fat raindrops on the window pane as he lifted the dusty curtain to peer down on the yard below. Darn it. Now if the landlady only came outside, he could signal to her. Connie, though, was hardly going to peg out her washing in this deluge, and all the while they waited for the rain to stop, there was more chance of Bill stirring.

Archie shared the rest of the cup of water with Bobby; the only means of getting more fresh water was from the pump in the yard outside.

Both boys sat with their backs against the wall near the window, occasionally one or the other standing to check outside to see if it had stopped raining. Finally it had, and they both smiled at one another as Bill turned over in his sleep. That rum he'd drunk the night before must have been strong stuff to knock him out this long.

But even though the sun was out, Archie realised the landlady would be kept busy at this time in the bar room below. At last he noticed Floss, one of the young maids, going outside carrying a wicker laundry basket of wet clothes. He dare not tap the window for fear of waking Bill so he just held up the note to the window pane in the hope it would be seen, but she was more interested in the task-in-hand and the young man who had just snuck up behind her wrapping his arms around her waist and planting kisses on the back of her neck. Archie felt a lump in his throat. There wasn't a cat in hell's chance now they'd get out of this room unless he found the key and to do that he'd have to dip his hand in Bill's pocket. The man still had all his clothing on from last night; he hadn't bothered to undress. He whispered to Bobby what he was about to do and warned the lad that if Bill awoke whilst he was trying to find the key he was to distract him and say there'd been someone tapping on the door so they were searching for the key as they didn't want to disturb him.

With bated breath, Archie tried to slip his hand into Bill's waistcoat pocket and though he grunted, didn't wake. He fumbled around but it was empty except for a bit of paper which he reckoned must have been a receipt for something or other.

There was nothing else for it, he'd have to delve into his trouser pockets and that was going to be very risky indeed.

The first pocket he tried felt very sticky and he dreaded to think what might have been in there; he felt a couple of coins and slipping them out handed them to Bobby, who slipped them into his own jacket pocket. Now they'd have to wait for Bill to turn over again in his sleep to gain access to the other pocket. But it was to be a long wait.

***

Cook was telling Albert all about what had happened when Alicia had lived at the house. It had all been hushed up at the time but as he'd worked there long enough she reckoned he'd had a right to know.

'So, you're telling me that Archie is Alicia's son?' He blinked in astonishment.

'The very one and the same.'

'That makes a lot of sense then, why the boy was drawn to the garden in the first place. His mother was just the same. Of course I knew something was amiss all those years ago but I thought that she'd been sent away, although I always wondered about that particular grave. I somehow knew it was something to do with her as I'd once seen her leave a bunch of violets there and she wept her heart out she did. She didn't notice me watching her—that wrapped up her in grief she was. I guessed it was her child that had died. But I never realised there were two boys.'

'Yes, that one only lived a matter of days and once the poor young woman discovered her parents planned on sending Archie to live elsewhere, she ran off with him and ended up in the East End of London until her recent death.'

'That were a sad business then. I had heard a whisper she'd passed away but I didn't realise she was living there. You kept the secret well, Margaret. Fair play to you, you're to be commended for that. Did any other staff here know about it?'

'Only Poker Face Mrs Linley.'

He grinned. 'Aye, you're right there and all, she is a right poker face!'

They both laughed until his face took on a serious expression. 'How'd you fancy stepping out with me next Sunday?'

The question fair near robbed her of her breath; it was many a year since a man had asked her that. 'Well, I don't know what to say. I have a day off this Sunday as a matter of fact.'

'Aye, I know. Polly told me!' he beamed.

'So, you'd already given it some thought, then?'

'Aye, I had and all. So will you?'

'Yes, I think I will, Albert. But where will we go?'

'Victoria Park would be nice this time of the year, we could go to the refreshment rooms.'

'I'd like that, really I would.'

'Maybe go out on one of the boats and all,' Albert said.

Cook was beginning to feel like a young girl again. This was all so exciting for her that she almost forgot all about Archie and she felt guilty for that.

***

Bobby nudged Archie. He was so tired from a poor sleep and lack of food that he'd almost drifted off to sleep.

'He's just turned over,' Bobby whispered.

Archie nodded and then slowly rose to his feet. If that key was in that pocket he was going to have to get it now before it was too late.

Gingerly, he went to slip his hand into the pocket, he closed his eyes as he fumbled around and felt the hard metal, slowly he went to tug it out. Bill grunted. Oh no, was he going to turn over or wake up? Then before he knew it, one more tug and the key was out in the palm of his hand. He stared at it so long that Bobby had to pull at the sleeve of his jacket to urge him to use it and get them out of there.

Both boys went to the door where they kept one eye on Bill. 'Now,' Archie whispered, 'there's the chance he might wake if he hears the click in the door and it opening. So be prepared to run for your life.'

Bobby nodded and then gulped. This might be the only chance they'd both get to escape and they knew it.

Carefully, Archie managed to get the key in the lock, but it wouldn't budge, the palm of his hand was perspiring so much it kept slipping off. 'It's rusty,' he whispered, 'too hard to turn.'

'Let me try.' Bobby looked at him hopefully. Archie knew the lad couldn't do it as he was smaller and in a weaker state, but he allowed him to try anyhow. He could have wept as he tried in vain to turn the key.

'One more try,' whispered Archie as Bobby moved out of the way, 'if it doesn't work, I'll replace the key in his pocket and we'll have to stay here.'

He wiped his hand on his trouser leg and, willing the door to open, he turned the key as hard as he could and felt a slight click. It was unlocking! He had butterflies in his tummy. Slowly, he opened the door and they were both on the other side.

'We'd better lock him in,' Bobby advised.

Archie tried his best but the key wouldn't turn any more on the other side of the door and they risked Bill waking up, so they quietly closed it and ran like hell down the stairs, through the crowded bar room until they were safely outside on the street, panting and hearts pounding like mad.

Now where to?

'Come on, let's get to the coaching inn, I need to warn Lucy she's in danger!' Archie said, knowing full well he might be in danger himself going there.

When they arrived out of puff after running continuously for fear of getting caught by Bill, Archie dragged Bobby around to the back door of the kitchen where they'd usually got their grub from. He knew Lucy might well be there but when he saw it was Cassie who was busy stirring a big pot of something on the stove, he pushed Bobby against the wall and said, 'Sssh, we'll have to wait until that woman leaves the kitchen. I don't know if we can trust her as she's well in with Casper.' Although he had thought, after hearing what Mr Casper had to say to Bill last night, that maybe he could trust the old fella after all. Well a damn sight more than he could trust Bill at least.

Archie took another peep in through the open kitchen door; Cassie had gone. Probably for a snooze in her armchair which she was prone to do while the food was cooking. He grabbed hold of Bobby's arm and drew him inside. 'We have to find Lucy,' he explained, but we can't risk being seen.' As they stood there the kitchen door opened slowly. Archie pulled Bobby to one side to hide behind a cupboard, and when they heard a lot of huffing and puffing and cussing too, Archie realised he'd been wrong, Cassie hadn't gone for her sleep as yet. Finally she left the room. They waited for a couple more minutes and as he was about to say something the kitchen door swung open and, to Archie's relief, Lucy was stood there.

She almost dropped the stack of dirty dishes in her arms when she saw them, but then she smiled and set the dishes down on the counter. 'What are you doing here, Archie? My aunt has been looking for you? And Bobby? I didn't know you two knew one another?'

Archie explained all that had happened and Lucy's eyes enlarged when he told her what Bill had said. 'Come with us to your aunt's house,' he urged, 'you're not safe here any more.'

She nodded and the three of them crept out of the kitchen and into the courtyard just as Casper and Smithy made an appearance. They were speaking to someone inside a coach that had just pulled up. Smithy's mouth fell open and he nudged Casper to attract the man's attention.

'When I say make a run for it, we all scarper!' Archie said. 'But try to keep together, understood?'

Lucy and Bobby nodded. Then the three children ran for their lives past the coach, out through the archway and onto the street outside. In the distance, they heard shouts from Casper and Smithy, but if they'd come after them, there was no way they'd have caught up as when Archie turned to look behind there was no sign of them. They didn't stop until they reached the alleyway leading to No Man's Land. Breathlessly, they stood against the cold brick wall and Archie said, 'Right…' he paused to inhale a breath and let it out again, 'in a moment or two we're going to run again until we get to your aunt's house, we'll go up the back lane as there'll be less chance of us being spotted that way.'

Archie was mindful that this was the spot where Bill had kidnapped him, so they needed to get away from there as quickly as possible.

'My auntie will be so pleased to see you, Archie,' Lucy said, with a big smile, but he could tell she was nervous and no wonder and all when he'd told her that Bill planned to kidnap her, too.

This was the most perilous part of the journey as the people who lived here were just as dangerous as Bill Brackley. 'Now we'll stick close together,' Archie said firmly, feeling he was responsible for them all.

Somehow they made it through the area and out into the alleyway that opened into the street where Mrs Harper lived. By the time they got up the back lane and were about to open the back gate, Archie fel a hand clamp down heavily on his shoulder. Oh no! Not Bill Brackley. The hand loosened and he turned to see Jacob stood there with a big leering grin on his face.

***

'Oi, yer little bastard, me ma's been looking for you! Where have you been? Don't like to see her upset.'

Archie didn't have time for any of this, so in temper, he kicked him in the shin.

'You'll pay for that! You'll see if you don't!' Jacob shouted at him, raising a fist, as the children made their way in through the back gate.

'Serves him right,' Lucy said. 'He's always been a big bully!'

When they arrived at the kitchen door, Bessie Harper was there to greet them. She almost broke down in tears when she saw Archie stood before her. 'Come in all of you!' she said, 'I've been so worried about you, Archie. Your Uncle Walter has been here and taken Duke home with him, he said I was to send word to him if you show up. What happened?'

By the time Archie had gone through the whole story of what happened to him and Bobby too, with a sprinkling of how Lucy was under the threat of danger while she remained working at the coaching inn, Bessie looked right worn out with the worry of it all.

'Well, you're quite safe here for time being,' she explained. 'You all look as though you could do with a good feed and a nice glass of me homemade ginger beer.'

Bobby was so overcome with the woman's kindness that he burst into tears and she cuddled him like he was her own son. Soon they'd all eaten a meat pie each with thick gravy and some mashed potatoes too and they sipped her ginger beer which was much better than the beer Bobby and Archie'd been forced to drink from pubs with Bill.

Later they sat in front of a roaring fire, Bessie rocking in her chair, her mind mulling things over.

'I'm trying to think how best to get word to your uncle, Archie,' she said. 'I could send Jacob over in the pony and trap?'

Archie didn't like the sound of that one little bit, he didn't trust the lad. 'Don't trouble yourself, Mrs Harper,' he said. 'Best thing would be for me to see Mr Baxter, the butler over at Nightingale Terrace. He'd want to help again, I'm sure.' Archie trusted that man with his life.

'Very well then,' Bessie said, with a look of uncertainty on her face. 'I do think we should contact the police though.'

That was the last thing Archie wanted at this moment, all he yearned for was to get home and for them all to be safe once again.

***

Bill awoke with a start, something wasn't right. He could hear voices drifting up the stairs and they seemed louder than usual. As his eyes came into focus he could see that the door was wide open and then they scanned the room. The little pair of bastards had gone! He leapt out of bed. Not again. They weren't going to get away with it this time.

Connie looked surprised to see him, she was collecting glasses in the bar area. 'Don't often see you up as late as this, Bill?' she enquired.

'What time is it then?' he scratched his head.

'Just gone two o'clock!'

He'd been asleep for a full twelve hours. Those lads could be anywhere by now. How did they get out of the room anyhow? They'd been locked in. He fumbled in his pockets for the key but it was nowhere to be found. 'Have you seen Bobby and Archie?' he growled.

'No, I thought they left with Flora?'

'Aye, they did but they had the good sense to return,' he lied. 'Flora's working the streets now. I couldn't stop her, I'm better rid. She always did have an eye for the men that one!'

Connie narrowed her gaze as if she didn't believe a single word that came out of his mouth. It was pointless hanging around, he needed to be off looking for them. If that Lucy was a friend of Archie's maybe he'd gone to the inn.

He found Casper as soon as he arrived, sitting on a wooden bench out in the courtyard as he watched a lad cleaning a coach in front of him.

'How do, Bill?' the old man said, as if he hadn't seen him for a while.

'The boys have got away again!' Bill growled. 'Have you got them hidden 'ere?' He narrowed his gaze as he noticed the old man tremble before him.

'N…no, Bill. To tell you the truth I was about to send me lad over there to your door to tell you what I seen this morning.'

'Oh, and what was that?' Bill quirked an interested brow.

'They was over here, me and the boy we saw them running off with that Lucy the young maid.'

Bill grabbed hold of the lapels of Casper's jacket, dragging him to his feet. 'And you didn't think to stop them?'

'How could I, Bill?' The whites of his eyes were on show as though he feared he'd get a good hiding from the man. 'Me old bones are rusty, I could never run after some kids.'

'That might be so,' Bill sneered, 'but what about me lado by there? He's young enough to be fleet of foot. He could have caught the buggers!'

'It weren't the right time, Bill. I was speaking to an important customer who had just arrived in his coach.'

As if Bill had suddenly come to his senses, he released the old man. 'Well if you see them again, let me know or the consequences will be dire for you!'

'Yes, Bill. Anything you say.' The man moved his hat back into position and sat himself back down again as if his feet would no longer take his weight.

Bill grinned. It gave him a sort of power knowing he could frighten the hell out of most folk, young and old. He turned and walked away back in the direction he'd come from, leaving Casper struggling to catch his breath as Smithy ran over to attend to him.

When Bill arrived at the back lane, the red-haired lad was there outside the bakehouse, standing against the wall chatting to some pretty sort. He stepped aside when he saw Bill as if slightly fearful of him.

'Seen that boy, Archie, have you?' he asked.

The boy gritted his teeth. 'The little blighter's inside the house with my mother, got a little kid with him and all and me cousin Lucy. Come to take him away, have you?'

Bill nodded with a big smile on his face. The lad seemed happy enough to give him up.

'Aye, well I'm bloody glad of it, he's a right little tearaway. I've tried to teach him a lesson a time or two. He kicked me in the shin earlier.'

'Don't worry,' growled Bill. 'He'll have his comeuppance sooner than he thinks...'

Chapter Fifteen

Bill headed towards the back of the house with purpose. Now that he knew he had one of Mrs Harper's boys on his side, he felt safe barging into the woman's house when she least expected it. He planned on taking them all by surprise.

He safely peered through the living room window to view a cosy picture of domesticity, the children huddled around the fireside while the old biddy rocked back and forth in her wooden rocking chair, all blissfully unaware of his presence. It would be like taking sweets from a baby.

'Your things are still nicely packed for you, Archie,' she was saying to the boy as Bill opened the back door ever so quietly lifting the latch, then he stood in the doorway his arm resting against the door jamb, in complete amusement of the situation before him. Daft bat hadn't even heard him enter.

Bobby looked up at him with a look of horror on his face. It gave Bill a great sense of satisfaction in the knowledge that he had that kind of power over him.

'Come along now then, boys, you're coming with me!' he said firmly.

Bessie carefully got out of her chair and reaching over to the fireplace, stood with a poker in her hand. Bill just laughed and pushed her down in the chair again. 'Ain't nothing you can do to stop me taking those boys,' he sneered. 'And given time, I'll take the girl and all!'

Suddenly the door leading to the hallway opened, causing Bill to turn around, and to Archie's relief, Harry stood there, with a look of fire in his eyes. 'Just what do you think you're doing to my mother?' he demanded.

Bill didn't flinch, but Archie knew who was coming behind him as it had all been pre-arranged. Mr Baxter was to tell the master and bring his coach over. Standing behind Harry was a well-dressed gentleman with two burly police constables.

Bill trembled, he didn't look so clever now. He scrambled to get away from the room and back out into the yard to make a getaway, knocking over a potted fern plant in its holder in the process, but the policemen had a strong hold of him. 'We've been after this one for a long time,' said the younger of the two, who had Bill's arm locked behind his back. 'He's been breaking the law sending lads up chimneys and soliciting women and now we can add kidnapping of children to the list! Which is an offence under the Offences Against the Person act of 1861! Section 56 to be precise!'

The inspector smiled and patted the young policeman on his back. 'We've trained you well, P.C. Parker, put him into the Black Maria but cuff him first.'

Archie watched in awe as Bill was led away. 'Bread and water for you from now on,' said the constable as he pushed him roughly out through the door.

The gentleman introduced himself to Archie as Mr Worthington, Mr Baxter's employer at the house Archie had delivered pies to.

'Thank you for bringing the police, sir,' said Archie.

Mr Worthington patted him on the head. 'I'm just glad you're out of danger, young Archibald. The inspector will have to take some details from you all and then my driver will take you back to your uncle. I'm sure Mr Baxter would be happy to accompany you seeing as how you've become good friends lately.'

Archie smiled and he watched as the inspector got out his notepad to take down some details. By the time Bessie had brewed up some tea for them all, and they'd had time to come to terms with all that had gone on, they were ready to leave and it was decided that Bobby would be taken to his mother at the same time, who no doubt was highly panicked by now.

Lucy had tears in her eyes as she said goodbye to both boys.

'Don't forget to write, will you, Archie?' she said wiping away a tear.

'No fear,' he said, planting a kiss on her cheek. 'I won't forget to write nor will I forget you, Lucy!' Then Archie thanked Mrs Harper for her generosity as she hugged him to her breast and, taking his belongings from her grasp, he left the house with both men and Bobby. He was going home at last.

***

Archie was sorry to say goodbye to Bobby, but it made his heart glad to see how happy Flora was to be reunited with her son. The woman looked pale as if she hadn't slept very much during the intervening days, but Archie promised he would stay in touch with them both, there was a bond formed between the three of them that he didn't want to break.

'Thanks for taking care of me Bobby,' she said, as they both waved off Archie as he left with Mr Baxter.

'And don't forget to keep writing those stories, Flora!' Archie beamed. 'And Nipper…take care of your ma!'

Bobby nodded as he wiped away a tear. It was hard for Archie to say goodbye to them both but there were others he would shortly be reunited with.

The journey back to the house seemed never-ending and as much as Mr Baxter tried to keep him going by chatting with him on the way, he just wished he could get home as quickly as possible. Wasn't it funny that now he referred to Huntingdon Hall as home when initially he'd dreaded going to live there?

As the coach drew up outside the house, the staff must have been waiting as Polly and Cook arrived on the steps shortly afterwards. Polly was wiping away a tear with her handkerchief and Cook had her arms open wide as she walked towards the carriage to greet him. But where was Uncle Walter?

He got so many hugs and kisses from both women that he needed to come up for air. Hearing a cough behind him, he introduced Mr Baxter.

'Well, it's been quite a journey for you both by the sound of it,' Cook said wisely. 'Come through to the kitchen and we'll have a nice cup of tea and something to eat.'

Mr Baxter smiled. 'That's very kind of you.'

'I hear that you're responsible for reuniting us with young Archie,' Cook said to the man.

Mr Baxter waved his hand. 'Oh, it was a pleasure, believe me.'

'Nevertheless Mr Baxter, you've done a fine thing in bringing him back to us, we have missed him so.'

When Archie got to the kitchen there was a surprise for him as Mr Featherstone and his tutor Mr Sowerberry were waiting to greet him. He was so overcome to see them that he could hardly speak for a few moments. But still, he wondered where Uncle Walter was. He was so disappointed he wasn't there to greet him.

They all sat around the pine table chatting and eating some jam tarts Cook had prepared. 'I knew you'd like these, Archie,' she enthused. Then turning to the others, 'The lad even brought some of these with him that a kindly neighbour had baked for him the first night he arrived.'

There was a lot of nodding and mumbling as everyone savoured the tarts, then quite suddenly there was a knock on the door which startled Archie.

'I wonder who that could be?' Cook looked a bit cross but behind Archie's back, she winked at Polly. 'Will you go and answer it please, Archie?' she asked.

He nodded, feeling very uncertain about it all. Gingerly, he drew open the door to see his uncle stood there. 'I'm so sorry I wasn't here to greet you but I was delayed at the picture framer's shop.'

'That's all right, sir.'

To his astonishment, his uncle shook his hand and gave him an awkward hug. 'Come through to the drawing-room,' he said. 'Excuse us a moment, everyone!' he shouted into the room.

They all nodded. Then he and his uncle made their way out of the kitchen and down the corridor. Why did his uncle want to see him in the drawing-room? When they arrived, his uncle paused outside the door.

'When I open the door, look up at the wall directly opposite you,' Uncle Walter said.

As the door slowly opened and Archie did as told, it robbed him of his breath. There, facing him, was the beautiful face of his mother staring down at him. Oh she did look pretty and all! Just like his ma looked every day, but a bit younger, not so tired looking, and right posh as well. She was wearing a beautiful shiny blue ball gown which looked like satin, around her neck was a string of pearls and in her hand she held a fan as she sat in a high back chair looking so peaceful and poised. The way she appeared in the painting made Archie think perhaps she was ready to attend a special ball at the house. The painting brought the woman he remembered to life, her sapphire blue eyes seemed to meet with his with great compassion as tears glistened in his own eyes.

'I hope I haven't upset you, Archie. But that's where I was today, arranging for this portrait of your mother to be especially framed for you. It's been in the family for a long time but the frame had broken. I wanted to put it back where it belongs.'

This time as Archie broke down, his uncle hugged him firmly to his chest and he realised the man was crying too as his shoulders wracked with grief. Finally, Archie looked up at him and said, 'You did this for me?'

'Yes, Archie, and for myself too. For years after my sister left here, I found it difficult to come to terms with her fleeing like that as we'd been so close, that's why on the rare occasion I visited your home I was hardly able to speak, I was so overcome by it all…'

At long last, Archie understood his uncle. The times he'd been quiet he wasn't being rude, he just didn't know what to say and that's why the first time he'd dined with him the man had blocked him out by reading a newspaper.

'Please forgive me, Archie, I've not been the best of uncles to you, but all that is about to change.'

Archie held on to him and for the first time in a long while felt really safe, loved and cared for.

'Thank you,' Archie said.

'Now I expect you'd like to see Duke?'

Archie nodded as he smiled through his tears. His faithful friend had helped get him through a difficult time.

***

A month had passed by and now Archie stood to gaze at the headstone in the small walled garden. So this was what had been behind that door in the brick wall all along. It had always felt such a mystery to him. The inscription read, 'Alfie Brooking born of this parish on August 12th, 1863. Taken too soon by the angels. Rest in Peace.'

He looked up at Cook and Mr Featherstone who were both stood there with tears in their eyes. 'Is this really my twin brother's grave?'

'Aye, it is and all, lad,' Mr Featherstone said, removing his cap as a mark of respect and clutching i to his chest.

Archie blinked. 'Then why was Alfie a Brooking and I'm a Ledbetter?'

Cook smiled. 'We think your ma invented the name so you could fit in with people at the East End and not be associated with Lord and Lady Brooking. You see, Archie, people might have put two and two together as she was in the newspapers as missing with her young son at the time, which of course was you. But from what I hear from Ginny, people knew anyhow. You are a Brooking though, your uncle has your birth certificate. This used to be an unmarked grave but your uncle has bought this new headstone and had an inscription engraved on it. He said there are to be no more secrets at this house.'

Archie swallowed. So much had happened of late and even since he'd returned to the house. He couldn't get over how missed and how loved he was. Even his Uncle Walter who wasn't a man of many words had been in tears, so moved to have him back home.

Cook handed Archie a bunch of violets. 'Mr Featherstone picked these from the garden as he remembered seeing your mother laying a bunch on the grave, would you like to place them there, Archie?'

He nodded and knelt down on the mossy verge to lay the fragrant flowers on the grave. It seemed strange knowing he had a brother lying beneath the earth, but as Cook had told him it was somewhere he could come to speak to the lad. He wished his mother was buried here too, but as it had been her wish to be buried near her final home, his uncle hadn't contested that. Secretly, Archie had wondered if his mother had fallen in love with a market trader who had the surname Ledbetter and that's why he was known by that name. Was he the man he had seen calling to his home late at night so long ago? Maybe he'd never know if his mother had found another romantic love during her lifetime, he so hoped she had though as it must have been lonely for a young woman with a young child, struggling to live in a new area. Ginny had hinted once that his mother'd had a special friend maybe she'd tell him when he reached that magic age of twenty-one. Meantime, he could now go by the name of Archie Brooking as that was his real name.

'We'll leave you in peace for a few minutes to reflect,' Cook said, as she turned and Mr Featherstone took her hand to walk out of the memorial garden. Archie had noticed how close the pair had become since he'd returned.

He stood there with tears streaming down his cheeks for a moment and he wiped them away with the embroidered handkerchief his old neighbour had given him the day of his mother's funeral. He'd always kept it in his pocket and Polly had washed it many times for him, and now given him the new one she'd embroidered for him, which he'd decided to keep for best.

The tears he wept were mixed ones. Today was going to be a good one as his uncle had arranged a special tea for him. Ginny and her family had been invited, Lucy and Mrs Harper and her sons, though Jacob had declined the invitation and Archie was pleased about that. Bobby and Flora were invited too. Cook was going to prepare a very special tea outside on the lawn with cucumber sandwiches with the crusts cut off, lots of fancy cakes and cups of tea and glasses of homemade lemonade. He couldn't wait to see everyone.

Uncle Walter had offered Flora and Bobby a place at the house with a job for Flora, but they'd declined as Flora was settled where she was and Bobby promised not to go off like that again without her knowledge. Bill was safely behind bars for the time being, so that was a load off Archie's mind.

However, one thing that puzzled Archie was that his uncle said someone else would be arriving that afternoon. A gentleman who had some good news for him. Archie couldn't for the life of him think what the news could possibly be.

Later at the house, Polly had laid out his clothes for him. There was one of those ruffled shirts he'd so hated wearing in the past because they were itchy, but now he didn't seem to mind at all and a new pair of breeches as Polly had said she'd sworn he'd grown a couple of inches since she saw him last. The outfit was set off with a long jacket with a velvet collar. He looked very much like his uncle now.

Polly gazed in awe. 'You look so dapper, like a right little lord!' she said, then she brushed away a tear.

For some reason, he felt like a right little lord and all, but this time he didn't mind one little bit.

He waited patiently by the drawing-room window to see the carriages arrive, it was a lovely sunny day though with a slight breeze in the air. He watched as Flora and Bobby, who were both dressed up to the nines descended from a hansom cab, with Simpkins there to greet them. Flora looked a proper lady with her hair swept up in a bun and she wore a damask blue cape and matching bonnet with a satin style dress beneath. Bobby wore a flat black cap and black jacket over a crisp white shirt and pencil-striped trousers. He did look a right toff, Archie had never seen him look so clean in all his life! And behind him was Mr Baxter. He dashed out to greet them.

Flora bent down and gave Archie a big kiss on his cheek, causing him to blush. 'I want to thank you so much for keeping Bobby safe for me,' she explained. 'I thought I'd lost him for good. I'm so glad that brute is locked away.'

Archie nodded. He wanted to forget all about Bill Brackley at least for today. 'All right, Nipper?' he asked looking at Bobby.

Bobby smiled. 'Yes, I'm happy being back at the house with Ma, I ain't never going out like that on my own again. It's not so boring now, the master has got me a tutor and I get to learn all sorts of things, just like you, Archie. I'm learning to read and write properly, too!'

Archie smiled. 'At least you'll never have to go up another chimney ever again!'

'How are things back at the house?' Mr Baxter asked.

'Very good, I'm settling in well, but I miss everyone so, particularly our morning chats!'

'So do I, Archie,' Mr Baxter said with a tone of regret in his voice. Then he swallowed as if he didn't want to cry. 'But we have to look at the good that's come out of this. At least we can still write to one another, I enjoyed your last letter so much. If I ever get lonely, I take out your letters and read them at night.'

Archie felt touched by that then whispered behind his hands, 'If Simpkins ever decides to retire, I'll ask Uncle Walter to take you on here…'

Mr Baxter chuckled at that remark.

As they carried on chatting, another carriage drew up taking Archie's breath away as he knew who would be inside.

Bessie Harper was helped out of the carriage first by the driver, she huffed and puffed a little as she stepped down and Archie could see she was wearing her Sunday best for the occasion. He'd never seen her look so grand. 'Archie!' she cried, 'Come here, lad! Let me see you!' He ran into her awaiting arms for a hug that went on for a long time and he could smell her fresh flowery perfume that reminded him so much of his mother. The warm-hearted woman had been like a mother herself to him.

He glanced behind her in expectation to see Harry descend the carriage with a big smile on his face. He had a lot to thank the lad for as if it hadn't been for him arriving when he had at the same time as the police, Bill might have got away with him and Bobby as Mrs Harper and her poker would have been no match for the man.

Harry shook his hand. 'Good to see you, Archie. Sorry, my brother can't come.'

'Don't worry about that, he won't be missed!' Archie chuckled and Harry smiled as if he understood all too well.

Then finally, Lucy stepped down from the carriage. She did look lovely and all as her chocolate brown eyes shone and she had the most beautiful of smiles. She wore a lemon silk dress that made her look so grown up, matched with the same colour bonnet over her lustrous chestnut brown curls. And around her shoulders, she wore a white lace wrap.

She stole Archie's breath away, she looked a proper little lady. He had some good news for her that he'd tell her later when they were alone. Uncle Walter was prepared to offer her a position at the house as a kitchen maid. He so hoped she'd accept, he didn't like the thought of her staying at that coaching house.

She smiled shyly when she saw Archie and he took her white-gloved hand in his to help her down from the carriage. He felt so much like giving her a kiss on that pretty little porcelain-like cheek of hers, but there were too many eyes on them; maybe later when he got her alone.

Finally, Ginny and her brood arrived in his uncle's carriage that he had sent especially to collect them.

The family burst out of the carriage and there was ever such an uproar as the kids ran hither and thither and Ginny and her husband, George, came over to greet Archie. His uncle had told her of all the latest goings-on.

'So, pleased you're all right, darlin'' she said, ruffling his hair that Polly had earlier so neatly gelled down into place with pomade but he didn't mind at all, he was only too pleased to see his old neighbours and especially the woman who had taken care of him at his mother's funeral.

The afternoon went by in a whirl and his uncle even said a few words to all the guests and staff about how pleased he was that all the children were safe and sound and that Archie was now back home where he belonged.

When they'd all departed, he led Archie into his drawing-room, there's someone I'd like you meet, young man,' he said, as he closed the door behind them.

Sitting in a high-backed leather chair was a clean-shaven man who wore a long dark coat, white shirt and black cravat. 'This is my lawyer, Mr Wilfred Peterson.'

Lawyer? Why was he meeting a lawyer? He didn't understand. 'Hello, sir,' said Archie.

The man smiled at him with a twinkle in his grey-blue eyes. 'Hello, Archie, come and sit down. I have some good news for you.' In front of him on the small table was a sheaf of papers and a fountain pen.

With some trepidation, Archie stepped forward and sat opposite the man with his uncle stood beside him. It appeared on closer inspection that the sheaf of papers Mr Peterson had in front of him might be some sort of document. 'Archie,' he said, 'you are about to become a very rich young man...'

Was this some kind of joke, a trick maybe? He looked at his uncle for confirmation. 'It's all true, Archie,' his uncle said. 'Your father was Sir Richard Pomfrey...'

Archie had heard that name as he was well known in this area. He'd heard Mr Sowerby speak about the Pomfreys, saying how the family owned a lot of land around there. He gulped, feeling hot all of a sudden. 'May I have a glass of water, please, uncle?' he asked all of a tremble.

His uncle smiled and poured him a glass from the jug on the table beside them and Archie took a sip as he carried on listening.

'I know up until now you had no knowledge that Sir Pomfrey was your father, it's been a well-kept secret. He has a son William, or I should say, had a son, William. He would have been your half-brother,' the lawyer continued.

'Would have?' Archie frowned. This wasn't making any sense to him whatsoever.

The man rubbed his moustache and hesitated for a moment as if he had some difficult news to impart. 'Unfortunately, he was killed in a riding accident a month ago when he fell from his horse, hitting his head on the ground. So you are the sole beneficiary. Apparently, when Richard Pomfrey died a few years ago, he left a codicil in his will stipulating that if anything happened to William the fortune was then to be inherited by his other son, Archie Brooking.'

Archie gasped.

'Don't you see,' said his uncle placing a hand of support on his shoulder, 'the man had made a point of acknowledging you as his son! He probably didn't do so back then not to hurt his wife and William, but now your brother has also passed away, there's no one left to hurt.'

Except for me, thought Archie.

This was too much for him to take in, he stood and looking at them both said, 'But I have no father!' He ran as fast as his legs could carry him to the grave of his twin brother and lay there sobbing on the damp mossy ground. He didn't know how long he'd lain there for when he heard a soft familiar voice say, 'Archie, it's all true. I fell in love with Richard and he with me.' He looked up to see the face of his mother stood beside the grave, but she wasn't as solid looking as she'd been in everyday life, he could almost see through her. He felt the light touch of her hand on his head and her warmth as she hugged him to her and then a golden glow reflected around her. She looked so beautiful, even more lovely than in the painting. 'I have my two boys together at last if only for a moment,' she said softly, in that sing-song voice of her's that he remembered so well. 'This house has had too many secrets for far too long.'

'Mama, I love you...' he sobbed as he felt her love encompass him. 'Take me with you and Alfie...' He stretched up his arms towards her.

'We'll be together one day, but not right now, there's work for you to do, a life for you to live,' she said softly, her words sounding soothing to his ears and comforting him deep down inside.

Watching as she began to disappear from view, he heard a final whisper, 'I love you, go back...go back...'

Remembering her words, he dried his eyes on his handkerchief and ran back to the house where his uncle and the lawyer were both still in the drawing-room, seated opposite one another, drinking a glass of brandy. His uncle smiled at his approach, it was if he was expecting something of the sort to happen, for Archie to return given time. 'Are you all right now, Archie?' he asked.

'I think so, Uncle Walter. It's all been too much for me to take in.' He flinched as he felt something wet and sloppy on his hand and noticed Duke there, he'd been licking him as if realising something had changed and Archie needed comforting.

'It's all right, Duke,' he said, dropping to his knees and burying his head in the dog's wiry fur.

His uncle smiled. 'That dog thinks a lot of you, Archie. He started whimpering when you left and I had to stop him from going after you as I realised you needed to be alone to think things through.'

'Did you try to follow me, boy? Did you really?' Archie realised how loyal the dog had been to him all this time.

Knowing that he was really Bill's dog, his uncle said, 'Duke had a lucky escape when he met you, Archie.'

Archie supposed that was true or else the poor dog could have still been under Bill's control, and although he'd never seen him hurt the dog, he wouldn't have put it past him. From now on he was going to have a good life with his best friend by his side.

Archie nodded, realising all would be well and, as he gazed up at the portrait of his mother on the wall, he could have sworn that she smiled at him.

Printed in Great Britain
by Amazon

48674786R00138